Bring Down
The Moon

Eva Le Bon

Published by
Chipmunkapublishing
PO Box 6872
Brentwood
Essex CM13 1ZT
United Kingdom

http://www.chipmunkapublishing.com

Second Edition with notes for Reading Groups and Trainees.

Edited by Obiz Ogbenns/ William Kettle

Art work by Zoe Grimes

ISBN 978-1-84991-646-2

Chipmunkapublishing gratefully acknowledge the support of Arts Council England.

Author Biography

This sensitively written novel is Eva Le Bon's first piece of fiction writing. From the tapestry of life including her experience as a psychotherapist, she has really loved letting her pen write this novel, with no rush over several years of her life, and has been intrigued by where it has taken her!

From post-war to present day Bring Down The Moon offers a moving account of how our everyday lives touch one another in unforeseen ways to make stories within stories. At times tear jerking and thought provoking Eva's story challenges us to keep on discovering our own pathway through whoever we think we are, whatever the cards of life have dealt us, as we write our own stories by the light of the moon.

'There is an enchanting tenderness about Bring Down the Moon and Eva Le Bon's ability to turn the darkest of moments into light is extraordinary. Keep this book on your bedside table, for it will whisper words of comfort and wisdom long after you have turned the last page.'

A.Bird
Freelance content editor, Munich

I dedicate this book:

To my parents, John and Margaret, and sisters Nanette and Rosanne, for a childhood rich in love and inspiration.

To Lucy and Charlie.
Thank you for your sparkle, for growing up with me, for more than I could ever put into words.

To David, my husband,
for being the heart and soul of my story
and

To Emma and Clare for being such gems.

CHAPTER ONE   NEW BEGINNINGS.

December 13th 2005.

'After all this time, you're here!'

The baby lay curled up, warm, sticky and weighty, on Lily's chest.

'You're beautiful,' Lily cooed to him.

'He is, and you're amazing Lily. I love you so much.' Lily squeezed Martin's hand. If only he knew how much she loved him; she could not have found a better partner if she'd searched the world. She looked sleepily back at him as she whispered, 'love you too.'

'There now, did you ever hear a pair of lungs like that? Are you going to be as big a fella as your dad? I'll just take another look at you.' Lily felt a warm, trickling, burning sensation between her legs as the midwife gently swabbed and soothed her.

'There you are, clean as a new pin. You're a great girl, so you are! Now, you be pressing the bell if you need the nurse to come? I'm away home to my bed, if I can get there that is! Well, bye-bye little fella, whatever they're calling you? '

'David, David Martin' Lily proudly announced.

'David Martin, very grand! Do you like that then, David?' The midwife smiled, 'I think he's saying he does. Now see that you give your mum some rest!' With that, the rosy-cheeked midwife was gone and suddenly there were so many questions Lily wanted to ask!

Moments later Lily wakened again. The room seemed extra cold and clinical in the night light and had that lingering smell of antiseptic, but for a smallish rural hospital it provided a more than adequate service.

'I'm so glad Lily that you came into hospital to have him,' said Martin.
'I know, I was just thinking the same. That nurse was fantastic wasn't she?'
'Absolutely! Reckon we got the best. Now then, darling, you must be shattered.' All of a sudden, as Martin stood up ready to go, Lily felt overwhelmed and tears were rolling down her cheeks.
'Darling whatever is it? O, goodness! Is that the time? Sorry, love, I really will have to go. They'll be on pins!'
'I know,'
'I'll probably just ring mum and dad tonight and I'll send a text to your dad and Olga. I'll ring round everyone else in the morning.'
'Good idea! Sorry, Martin, I don't know why the tears. I think it's just 'baby tears' and I'm tired and sore. Now then, off you go, and get some sleep. Have you got that de-icer?'

Two minutes later Martin was gone and Lily reached for the tissues as she heard the door clang shut behind him. She hadn't expected to be quite so weepy: a little boy, how wonderful! How could she ever explain to Martin the mixture of emotions she was feeling; so happy, relieved but also sad.

'Gracious me, are you OK? Whatever's the matter? You'll be waking the neighbourhood!' the nurse said as she came rushing in hearing Lily's sobs and the baby crying.
'I want my mum.'
'Visiting time isn't until 2.00 pm tomorrow. Never mind you wanting your mum, I reckon this little man is saying he wants his too. Perhaps we'll just try a feed?' In the milky twilight, the stinging pull of David's first long suck brought stars to Lily's eyes, and a jarring back to motherly duties.

'Ouch! So that's what you think?' The nurse helped him settle on the nipple, bringing a gradual smile back to Lily's face. How comforting and reassuring the nurse was in those early moments, especially when following the feed she gathered baby from Lily's breast with:

'Now come on little one. Come with me to the nursing station, that's right! We'll look after you, give your mum here, a proper chance to sleep.'
Lily dried her tears and, muttering her thanks, she turned to her diary.

13.12.05   At last, a son, David, he's gorgeous, safe and well all 6lbs 8 ounces of him! We reckon we can see us both in him, as squidgy as he is.
Been feeling really weepy, wish mum and Aunty Fleur were here too. They'd love him to bits. Holding him is the best thing in the world.

Lily put her pen down and snuggled under the covers. She closed her eyes and soon was thinking: 'It's Tuesday. Ah, 'Tuesday's child is full of grace.' Lorne and Isles district hospital, what a lovely place for David to have been born!'

5 years later.

The stunning coastline of Budleigh Salterton forms the western most section of the Jurassic coast, with its unique Red Devonian Sandstone rising from the water on either side of the cliffs.
'Call in again when you're next visiting.'

Another drop into the oil burner, another happy customer and a gentle citrus fragrance of oranges and roses started to fill the shop.
'Very tasteful,' Polly thought, a subtle way of masking the slightly stale smell of second hand clothes and of introducing something less overbearing than Sandra's squirts of 'fresh linen!' Polly smiled across at her. There she was, busy helping a customer.

'It really suits you...you might need it taken in a bit. There, I'll just hold it for you. Yes, that would make all the difference.'
'How much?'
'£22.50, it's not often we have an Ann Balon dress in: it'll look good dressed up or down, with evening shoes or worn casually with boots.'
Five minutes later, the auburn haired lady was gone along with the necklace that Sandra had helped her to choose.

'What a busy day it's been! Are you getting off straight away Sandra? Would you like that extra five minutes now as I just remembered you said you wanted a chat and I'm not in again until Wednesday?' Ten minutes later, with the shop sign turned to 'Closed', Polly and Sandra were enjoying welcome mugs of sweetened tea. Polly knew just the way Sandra liked it!

'I found this under a heap of clothes inside that old suitcase over there' said Sandra.

'Wow! I see what you mean. That's a real one off; do you think we should have it valued?'

'No. Well yes I know what you mean, but no. It's this; this is what I was hoping to speak to you about.' Sandra opened the ebony box, richly inlaid with mother of pearl. Carefully, she clicked a lever inside the box.
'Goodness, that's the sort of thing you see on the Antiques Road Show! Mind you it's probably not old, old, but still, a box with a secret compartment, you did brilliantly to spot that.'
'Yes but wait Polly, just look what's inside!'

When Sandra pulled out an old book, a few loose leaves fell out which she straightened and replaced neatly behind the cover. On the top was a drawing, a sketch done in pen and ink showing a lady with two small children standing by a tree. By some miracle Sandra, had found herself flicking through the pages, engrossed.

'What is it, some sort of manuscript? Have you read it yet?'

'No, I've just flicked through the pages so far. It looks like it's someone's memoirs. Apart from the beginning, it's written almost completely as reflections headed in sections, perhaps ready to be turned into chapters.

"Bring Down The Moon", nice title, might even belong to someone famous,' Sandra mused.

'Now you really are romancing. Mind you, I wouldn't mind being on that road show, I used to like Michael Aspel! I've got some time over the next few days, so you never know I might just read it. I'm intrigued already. Certainly makes you wonder where it came from, and if it is very personal then what are we going to do with it?'

Once back home, ready for an early night, Polly climbed into bed with a glass of wine and picked up the manuscript. The evenings could seem long these days since Philip's untimely death, so it was going to be good to have something to read: in fact ideally she'd finish it by Wednesday.

Polly looked at the sketch with the picture of the lady and the children; it seemed somehow even more haunting, more troubled in the bedroom twilight. Polly turned the picture over. Clipped onto the back of the drawing was what looked like the writing for the sleeve of a book, maybe it was intended to be published after all.

Synopsis

Following the tragic loss of their two year old son: Christopher, Dr Andrews and Elizabeth reluctantly leave their dales home: 'Springhill', for New Zealand. Five years later they return with two little girls: Maria and Fleur, and find the moon once more over their doorstep.

Straddling the genre of romance and family saga, the novel opens post-war and soon becomes an account of the heroine: Fleur's story. It is a story of honesty, and veiled truths with the intensity of emotions as two sisters marry two brothers. 'How wonderful to have such closeness,' Fleur thinks, but is it?

Fleur changes through the years, arriving at that place in time we have all trodden: the unknown. As Fleur journeys, the views are spell binding, the road so rocky, her feet bleed and now in her advancing years, she seeks a simpler life, completing her journey by the shores of East Devon. Many a reader's nerve might be touched by the layering of stories within stories, highlighted through the eyes of Annie, the doctor's housekeeper; Fleur, the heroine, and Father Francis on his death bed.

Eerily, we sometimes catch the broken cobwebs of time through an overarching commentary. Could it be the voice of the moon above, weaving its way in and out of the story?

C1:   Home-making.   1954.

'It's true; we just have ten days to prepare for their return.'

'Did you hear that? Dr Andrews and his wife Elizabeth are coming home, after all this time.'
'I can hardly believe it, when did you hear?'
'Who told you? Are you sure?'

Annie, holding on to her hat, as if keeping the lid on the flurry of questions from Ivy and Janet, carried on:
'Will it be five years? Aye it is that, that's an awful long time. Will we need to be sure we give them a warm welcome, then?'
Annie's upward inflection had that charming lilt that belonged to the highlands, and she had Great Aunt Edith to thank for her way of framing things as questions of a kind.

'Quite a legend,' Annie recalled to herself, as her mind wafted back to Great Aunt Edith, and her homemade scones.
'Five years, already,' she thought. Time had passed 'awful quick!' There was a spring in her step as she walked on her way and smiled to herself as she thought about the corner shop and Ivy! It really was as good a place as any for village gossip, but poor Ivy, if there was a wrong end of the stick to get, she'd get it!

Annie loved the dales around her; the undulation of the hills and dry stone walls, the limestone cliffs. She loved the wild 'Wuthering Heights' moments of biting turbulence where life seemed on an edge; but most of all she loved the character-istic sound, that haunting bleating sound of sheep which seemed to reach her wherever she was, striking an emo-tional chord in her in much the way that bagpipes could. This was home to Annie, at least since she was eight years of age.

'I don't know,' mused Annie out loud to herself, as she started to climb the hill 'forty six years here and still a newcomer!'

Hefty and comely as she was in build, Annie's sparrow like legs carried her well and her greying sandy hair was usually caught back in a neat bun at the nape of her neck and topped, when outside, by a neutral coloured woolly hat that rarely changed with the weather; she had a handsome face with fading freckles and soft grey twinkling eyes. Annie loved walking, or 'strolling' she called it. She loved the smells, the sounds, the air feeling fresh on her face and was already starting to think of the fire she'd be lighting once back home.

Annie could make anything sparkle: home making was her forte and she knew herself well, all her little foibles! She knew there were times when she needed to be quiet and rest, perhaps drained from her physical graft and having listened endlessly to someone's story. It wasn't just 'Annie the hard worker and good listener,' because she equally would take her turn; enjoy having a favour done for her, and would chatter away about this and that, glad someone was listening to her too. She was quick to banter, and had a 'bend you up double' sense of humour; but, first and foremost, Annie was a practical person and that helped her enormously to see an order of priorities that kept life simple.

Brier cottage had been home to Annie and Harry since the start of their marriage in 1920. It was at the end of a terrace of three cottages and had open views in every direction. Annie and Harry always liked growing things and, from the start, kept pots of herbs in their yard way for cooking. Perhaps Annie had picked up the idea from her grandmother who had used herbs for concocting old-fashioned medicinal remedies. The croft of land had been tenanted to Annie and Harry unexpectedly and they had taken it in their stride. Within six months of the land becoming theirs, Harry had fixed boundary walls and fences in place and Clover and Nancy moved in, along with the hens. The livestock varied only a little over the years and usually consisted of at least one milking goat, six hens and Clover, the donkey: the village children loved her and each year someone would enjoy being 'Mary' in the Christmas play so having a special chance to ride her.

Annie was a bit of an Earth Mother to everyone: the one putting on the tea parties in the village hall during ration time and the one behind the food for the summer fete.

'How do you do it, Annie? That's what I'd like to know; how do you make a tin of corn beef stretch to feed an army? Will you show me how to darn nylon stockings?' Eileen with her eight children knew she could ask Annie anything. She loved Annie for she could learn from her and it was so endearing, the way Annie had no problem also sharing with her the odd time when her own Yorkshire puddings had flopped.

In 1945 when the message came over the wireless that the war had ended, Annie, 'the strong one', collapsed. She had been steady as a rock for everyone whilst the war was going on but once it was over the relief of the news sent her legs to jelly. She was so grateful to see loved ones, safe and home but at the same time was sensitive to the huge losses around; those neighbours who were not lucky enough to see their loved ones walk back in through the door. There had been six families in and around Pen-y-dale who had lost their sons to war. 'What a lot the war has to answer for, Annie thought as she neared home.

Thinking about the doctor and his wife's homecoming, had triggered a cascading of memories. She remembered the times when in spite of all the hardships, the villagers could be so amazing! At harvest time, Annie would find half the community on her doorstep ready to help gather in the crops in exchange for taking some home with them. What a happy arrangement for everyone! It was during that time that a tall, gangly lad with an attractive, off beam smile arrived at Annie's door looking for work.

'Well, blow me down I was just thinking of you. Hello, Frank'
'Mornin,' Annie. Good job I called by after lunch; some o' back fence were down so I've done a make shift job for you until Harry sees to it, but at least it'll save you having Clover and rest o' 'em wanderin'.'
'Ah, Frank! What a thoughtful lad you are! Would you be coming on in for a cup o' tea?'
'No, you're rit, better get back.'
'OK, Frank, then we'll settle up with you tomorrow, and I'll be singing your praises to Harry.'
'See you soon Annie. Go, warm up.'

There was something about Frank's expression, the uncertainty in his voice, the way he looked to you for reassurance: a sincerity that really tugged at Annie's heart.

'They call me Frank Horner, Ma'am' Annie repeated in a quiet semi 'out loud' way as she recalled the first time she had met him with: 'Julie Tinsdale,' Annie muttered, as she remembered. Julie was a polite young girl who was always very kind to her son: Frank, born to her when she was only sixteen, a truth he himself never knew, but how he loved his 'Aunty Julie'. As for Harry and Annie, they never once regretted taking Frank under their wing; they knew the length and breadth of his limitations, but a more willing pair of hands, they could not have hoped to find anywhere.

Once through the white gate, Annie fiddled with the second key in the lock and opened the heavy stable door that lead into the front room.
'There we are,' she sighed pulling off her coat and shoes. She was pleased to be home; still a bit 'out of puff' from the

walk up the hill, her feet felt the relief of the comfy slippers she kept by the fireplace. The fire was just about 'in,' ready for another shovel of coal and a couple of pieces of wood. Annie stood beside it for a while, having a warm, it would soon be crackling away.

Annie sneezed. The front room was a potpourri of smells: accumulations from cooking and baking, from cut flowers, from the fire, the cat and polish. A n n i e was great with the duster, rubbing on and rubbing off and she had collected some well-loved pieces of furniture over the years. There was granny's welsh dresser and barley sugar legged dining table and Aunt Edith's rocking chair, that still needed a bit of re-upholstering.
'Come on Smokey, off the chair you go, little scamp that you are!'

Annie loved the peace of Brier cottage, the homely atmosphere of the clock ticking whilst Smokey curled up in the corner of the window seat, washing himself. She loved rocking in her chair with time to think things through slowly without any rush; she enjoyed looking out from where she was sitting at the view, she could see as far away as Pendle Hill. How she missed her mother: even with her outspokenness! Annie would smile, hearing her mother saying:

'To think Annie, after all those times I had to get on to you about the state of your room, you could turn into such a good wee housewife! Where did you get those chintzy covers from for the settee? I dare say they cost a bob or too! Did you run short for the windows?'
What a shame! Annie's mother could never see their differences, how Annie might simply have not wanted matching curtains! But for all the irritations even after all this time, when the phone rang Annie half expected and wished it to be her mam.

'Ah well' Annie sighed and interrupted the helpless feeling she was starting to have about her mother's sad life with 'just one of those things!' thoughts, as she got up and went to make herself an Earl Grey and settled in Harry's large easy chair at the side of the fireplace.

'Thank goodness she had curtains and things to bother about. I think I'd have needed a distraction too if I had been in her shoes.' She sighed a long 'aged six' sigh as she reached out to the photograph of Harry on the table by her side. She picked it up, gave it a perfunctory kiss, and put it back firmly. 'Now where's that list o' mine?'

Annie loved her Earl Grey and she loved her Harry; she could set her watch by him. He said he'd be back by five o'clock and five o'clock it would be. His walk in the hills would take him another two hours she reckoned, which gave her plenty of time to put the casserole into the oven and do her 'to do' list for the doctor's home coming. She felt proud of Harry; he was solidly reliable and it was so wonderful that he was home safe and well from the war; he had seen so many of his regiment killed.

Decorating: Remind Harry and Tom

Laundry: Curtains, towels, linen

Bedrooms   Bedding and eiderdowns air

Cot   Prepare

Baking Apple pie and scones

In between writing her list, Annie was daydreaming as she emptied the washing tub, set the table, washed and stacked a few dishes in the sink, put the vacuum on over the downstairs carpets, popped up- stairs to run a comb through her hair and powder her nose; all in time to have that extra stir of the casserole before Harry's return.

Her first meeting with Harry was by the tombola at the village fete in the summer of 1919. Try as she could, Annie could not recall the first words they had exchanged, but the feelings were as if it all happened yesterday. Annie had often wondered how she would know when the right man came along; in idle moments she had even rehearsed the occasion, what she might say to him, how she might look abashed! In the 'here and now' of that coy moment, it made her feel a little light-headed and she had found herself tongue-tied and overcome. It was two days before her birthday: July 15th and about four weeks after the summer fete when Harry walked Annie home after a chance meeting one afternoon.

'Annie, I was wondering if you would not think it too forward of me...'
'Yes, Harry?' Annie intervened with encouragement.
'Would you care to walk out with me to the brass band parade? They are playing on the village green in the early evening tomorrow?'

Harry was a patient man and had a twinkle in his eye that helped you to see the funny side of something, and Annie absolutely loved the fact that as tall and handsome as he was, he was no rover and quite shy in some ways. She knew there were times when she could irritate Harry like mad with her 'bees in her bonnets' but he usually found a way of settling the buzz and had the knack of helping her down from that occasional 'high horse' too. Fundamentally, Annie felt at home and valued; he appreciated all she did - it was simple. Harry on the other hand had a way of putting his foot into things, but loved to see how he could stir Annie into lots of laughter and he knew she knew that his intention was to always be a solid support to her.

The casserole she had placed in the oven was bubbling away and Annie put an embroidered cloth on the card table that settled by a roaring fire, ready for Harry's return. Annie rarely heard the grumbling Harry did as actual grumbling (a bit like her mother's 'nagging' perhaps); it just went through a sieve in her head that turned into light amusement. Half an hour later (the timing for the casserole was perfect), Harry was home.

'Hungry dearie?' Annie asked as she placed his hot meal on the table.

'Like starving Russia,' he replied, and in listening mode Annie let Harry enjoy his meal and tell her all about his day. Harry always became engrossed in the re-telling of his own stories, so that when Annie rose to her feet; Harry noticed it as 'abruptly!'

"O, dear, what's wrong? Whatever has happened? I can tell from your face. Are you upset pet? No? Do I need to go and put on a collar and tie, smarten up before you tell me?"

Annie had moved from being irritated to cackling out with her infectious giggle: 'What are you like?'

Annie relayed the story of Dr Andrews and Elizabeth's imminent return to Springhill, including her encounter with Ivy Pickles.

'You mean that nosy parker woman, the one who looks pale and constipated all the time?' Fond as she was of Ivy, Harry's description was perfect.

'That's wonderful news! Go on, pet, tell me more,'

Harry followed Annie into the kitchen,

'OO, you old rogue you,' Annie laughed as she felt Harry's hand tap her on the backside as she bent down to take the apple pie from the oven.

'Rogue! Who me? Now you can't help a husband taking advantage of his good woman's 'apple pie position!'

Annie laughed, 'you, monkey, you.'

'There's only the two of us here,' Harry persisted.

'On with you, old rogue, that you are!' Annie chuckled to the monkey sounds Harry had started to make.

'Now, go on, what were you saying as I followed you to the kitchen? You let me tell you all about my boring day and held back your important news about the doctor's return. Now isn't that my Annie for you, always puts herself last.'
'Mind, don't go making any saint of me, Harry Lowther,' Annie replied smiling,
'I just needed time to get a word in edge ways!'

Annie continued to tell Harry about the surprise telegram they had had that morning all the way from
New Zealand. It simply stated:

DR GAVIN AND ELIZABETH RETURNING HOME FRIDAY 24th SEPTEMBER WITH OUR TWO LITTLE GIRLS: MARIA AND FLEUR. LOOK FORWARD TO COMING HOME. WILL CALL YOU SOON AS WE ARRIVE IN DOVER.

'Dover. Friday. Two little daughters! Well I never, that's amazing! What are they called again? How old are they? Does either of them look like little Christopher?'
'Harry,' Annie interjected, 'what are you like? I only know as much as you do, we will just have to be patient'.
'Come on...look at you now, mop them up'. Annie relaxed a little, as she felt Harry's strong warm arms around her.
'It is wonderful news, Harry.'

'You loved that little boy,' Annie found Harry's large handkerchief, soft and comforting, she kept twining it round her fingers like a worry rag. What a long time it had been!

Five years had passed since the doctor and Elizabeth had left the sleepy village of Pen-y-dale, following the tragic death of their little boy Christopher who had died at the age of two from leukaemia. He was a beautiful child with dark eyes and silky dark hair just like his father's. He was bright and sunny, and could be very funny at times. Annie had often baby-sat for Dr Gavin and Elizabeth on their special occasions. Christopher's tragic illness came as such a blow to the couple and the whole village.

'Do you remember when Christopher was born, Harry?'
'Remember? I do, you put the card in the window.'
'That's right. The card used to mean 'home visit', and none of the doctors liked seeing it there, because it meant 'more work': an interruption to an already busy morning; they'd have to stop the car, come inside to collect the details. What a surprise that day! Remember how the doctor came running in?'
'I do, and he was fairly bristling, expecting an emergency, and instead.'….
'Baby Christopher had been born, safe and sound!' Harry finished off for Annie completing that shared memory, and he watched on tenderly as she walked over to the welsh dresser to take out the photograph album. She knew exactly where it was kept.

'Now Annie, mind you don't go upsetting yourself.'
'Ah! Look at him, all that hair, at the christening. I reckon he looks about two on this one.'
'Got some chocolate on his face on this one,' said Harry doing his best to lighten things up a little.

'Two years, two weeks this one says on the back of it.' Annie turned over another page of the album.

'Ah, see here how gaunt Elizabeth looks and that's two months before they lost the wee soul. So sad.'

Thursday, 9 September 1948, that was one of the saddest days.

It seemed beyond contemplation to think that this perfect family could have their own major tragedy in full view of everyone. Dr Gavin was, after all someone who everyone looked up to and who people expected to go to for their own treatment and Elizabeth, a vicar's daughter should be consoling others rather than receiving condolences herself.

'I just thought it was so sad to see them go all that way away to New Zealand,' said Annie.

'I know, it just gave them a chance for a breather. Village life can be so…'

'Claustrophobic!'

'That's the one. Now come on Annie, it was a long time ago and we've to welcome those two little girls. So put that book away.'

Harry's tone of voice still had that warm ring of his father's Geordie accent: 'tell you what pet, there's a bit of clearing behind that rhubarb. How about us having a little piece there for our Christopher? We could put some rosemary there for remembrance and forget-me-nots, alongside the buttercups and daisies.

'O, Harry, how do you do it? I can just imagine those wee girls skipping and playing there. They never need know the significance of it, at least not until they're old enough to understand,' she sighed.

'Just going upstairs a moment to freshen up.'

'That's my girl', Harry replied. He knew Annie was such a brick for so many people and it saddened him to picture her behind the bathroom door on her own crying, yet he reckoned sometimes, when he saw tears well up in her, she sometimes needed him to step aside and let her have that private space.

Annie had had the heartache of several miscarriages before having Billy and Susan and knew how difficult it could be talking to people. Annie finished combing her hair; she had cried enough; she had things to do and, ever practical, tuned in to what Harry would say; 'That's life for you!' and with that thought she smiled, stood up taller and walked downstairs.

Soon Annie was recalling to herself five years ago, but in practical ways. The replacement young doctor and family hadn't taken to the country practice but had soon been replaced by a much more suitable locum. Doctor McFarlane came with a reluctance to become attached and embedded but had a sincerity of spirit as well as a good sense of humour that warmed the people of Pen-y-dale to him. He had no intentions of making sweeping changes and suited the dear practice house, Springhill, with its stone steps leading down to the surgeries. He was often seen, time and weather permitting, striding out with trousers tucked into his boots and aided with a much loved walking stick and with a familiarity of purpose, as if he had walked the paths before.

No one knew the old doctor well or what became of him after he left. Perhaps he wanted it to be like that! He was content and that made all the difference. He loved nothing more than to look out on a clear day from the morning room window and see across as far out as Pen-y-ghent.

C2: Reflections.

Elizabeth and Gavin had been thinking about whether they should return along with their little girls or whether they should look again for a new beginning. However, in the end it didn't feel as though they had had to make a decision; they simply found themselves being drawn back as if by an invisible moon to the place they had loved so much. The five years away had given them the time for Elizabeth to have her breakdown in peace. The offer of New Zealand had seemed perfect timing for them, and they had left with no expectations, simply deciding to take things quietly and slowly without drawing too much attention to themselves; difficult one would think for such a naturally distinctive couple, the doctor with his refined good looks and darling Elizabeth with her quiet disposition, intelligence and femininity.

Elizabeth and Gavin were believers in a 'good life,' but not particularly in organised religion. Elizabeth had grown up in a vicarage, so was used to an ever open house, many 'bring and buys', hymns, weddings, funerals, flowers, cups of tea and scones!

Elizabeth's cousin 'Robin' was renowned to have caused enough trouble for anyone, and maybe that story about him had contributed to her inability to swing along through life as much as her schoolgirl peers had done. Robin would frequently be on the edge of trouble with the police and always seemed to dance with bringing shame upon the family. Elizabeth was very close to Robin as they grew up but adolescence seemed to bring gaps in their relationship. Conflict was something to be avoided.

Way back in Gavin's Grandpa's day the family was Roman Catholic but Gavin's father had rebelled against going to church and distanced himself from his close ties with his family. Not surprising then that the young Gavin grew up amidst this puzzle, so took a betwixt stance to everything.

Gavin remembered his grandparents well and their routine of going, without question, to Sunday morning Mass. He loved them both so much- what characters! He loved the way grandma would daub lavender water behind her ears and the way they processed into church slowly and steadily in their 'Sunday best,' inclining their heads towards people in recognition of them. He loved the way they would kneel with their arthritis to genuflect as they entered the same pew each time. Gavin got used to what to expect; the rituals, the smells, smiles and nods. He noticed that they even spoke with their aitches on Sundays!

Grandpa was quite a character. He always seemed at least eighty in Gavin's mind. He was a burly man, with trousers that came up to his armpits held in place by braces. His hair was cut short over his ears, almost on a level with his fringe and his head looked like it was designed for a military cap. He had a fine voice but used to embarrass Gavin by singing as loud as he could. Volume seemed the most important sign of a good voice to him.

Grandma, on the other hand, thought that she had a beautiful voice, but as modesty was of utmost importance to her she would start her singing so very quietly you could hardly hear her, then, as she drew strength and forgot the modesty, her voice would be heard warbling to notes sustained just a little longer than anyone else's! She used to like to think she knew best and Gavin could not explain to himself why, even now, when he thought of her and her good intentions, a tear of affection could well up inside of him. Grandma would look at young Gavin so tenderly; maybe missing the close relationship she once had with her own little son. She would say:

'And how's your father doing, expect he's busy?' Gavin was always sensitive enough to know not to report back about going to Mass to his dad.

There were times when Gavin was a bit bored with some of the rituals: the standing up and sitting down that seemed to happen every Sunday. He had little understanding of what things were supposed to mean and instead picked his nose, hiding them in rows under the pew around where grandma was sitting. But all that aside, there was something about the stirring of the candles, the mysticism of incense that he found heady. Indeed, spiritually, he felt quite drawn towards it and this feeling would remain with him all his life.

'You never hear anyone speaking Latin do you?'

'Don't be silly Gavin,' said grandma dismissively.

'It's a dead language,' they choroused in catechism like unison.

'Very strange,' thought Gavin imagining Latin lying on its side covered in leaves.

At the close of Mass when everyone filed passed the priest, it always felt that the priest spent an extra bit of time with the Andrews as if they were rather special. Perhaps they were held in high regard or maybe that was just the memory that Gavin chose to keep with him of those special 'grandparent' times.

And so, from their different backgrounds, Gavin and Elizabeth brought ideas of how to be together and have their family. They spoke little of religion, because they did not wish it to be a big issue between them. In fact, they found they were of like mind about many things. Perhaps the strengths of the powerful opinions that went before them helped them arrive at their middling path. They did not feel anti organised religion and were supportive of a number of churches and good causes; appreciative of the work they did. Some might say Dr Gavin and Elizabeth found their kind of faith through the love of the countryside but neither of them ever forgot the value of the bustling towns and villages close to where they had grown up.

COUNT DOWN TIME.

In the five years that they were away, the doctor and Elizabeth spent most of their time at the practice in New Zealand. By the time they left, they were well loved, for who wouldn't love Dr Andrews and Elizabeth? Gradually and methodically Annie went through the list. Under her close supervision Tom and Harry redecorated and painted Springhill throughout in neutral shades so that it smelt freshly laundered and was ready for new curtains to be hung at the windows.

'That's grand, just needs a few wee touches.'

'Then it'll be right', and within a minute of that thought, Harry found himself clambering up the ladder and into the loft.

'Goodness, you could open a shop with everything that's up here,' he said.

'We just need the warming pan, dear. I think it's in a square crate that has the silver in it, wrapped in newspaper; I'll come up.'

'O, no you won't, pet,' Harry quickly replied seeing all the memorabilia of Christopher that was up there. 'There now, found it.'

It took Harry a few minutes longer to actually find it but at least he'd managed to curtail more distress for Annie. Harry was very protective of her: sensitive to the struggles she had had as a child growing up in such fear of her father. She had been so uncomplaining during the struggles of having their family when she repeatedly miscarried, and could never speak of the stillborn baby that they had had themselves. It was almost as if it had never happened.

'That's grand. Looks just right.'

'Back just where it belongs,' agreed Annie as she hung the polished warming pan in the inglenook fireplace.

'Aye, It's looking like 'home' again for them.'

AT LAST THE DAY ARRIVED

'They're here,' shrieked Annie as she straightened her pinafore and stroked her hair back from her face.
'Please Harry, come and answer the door with me.'
'Well, hello,' they simultaneously said in their different ways.
'My, you're looking well.' Annie said as she looked admiringly at Elizabeth. What a presence she had! Annie touched and straightened her own hair, as she looked at Elizabeth's now longer hair, tied and caught loosely in a chignon. 'Quite the lady,' she found herself thinking.

Gavin and Elizabeth loved their welcome afternoon tea and settled the little girls into their chairs side by side.
'They're gorgeous, so they are,' said Annie.
'So this is Maria,' she looked a picture with her jet-black hair and curly eyelashes.
'And this must be Flora?'
'No, Fleur.'
'What did you say?'
'Fleur, it's French for flower.'
'Oh, that's lovely.'

Fleur was as fair as Maria was dark, with the deepest of blue eyes. Annie was right, as different as they were, they were both just beautiful. There was eighteen months between them. Maria was just about to have her fourth birthday, whilst Fleur was two years old.

'Goodness, there must be a lot for us to catch up on. You've worked so hard getting things ready for us Annie. We didn't know what to expect, with having been away so long and the house having been occupied by others.'
'Will I take you upstairs and show you your rooms?' Annie asked with warmth and concern in her voice. What would it be like for them seeing Christopher's room again?

'Gavin, darling: Come, look,' Elizabeth called.

'Look what they've done with…' her voice trailed away as Elizabeth was changing the course of her words.

'Maria, isn't this lovely? Ah! Look at that, bless her she's lined her toys in a row in her bed already.

You are a lucky girl to have such a pretty room aren't you?'

Maria was beaming and Gavin passed Elizabeth a tissue, gently rubbing her arm.

'You've made it so charming Annie! Thank you. Thank you so much.'

'O, you're welcome Doctor'.

'She's been run off her feet you know, my Annie, so worried about your coming home to all the memories of Christopher, that's why she's been…'

'Shush!' Embarrassed, Annie was trying to stop Harry putting that size 15 straight into it.

'Decorating away with that driving force of hers, making things fresh and clean for you.'

There was something about Harry and his indiscretions that was so refreshingly honest, and so apart from a moment's tension, when the penny dropped for Harry that bit later than it did for everyone else, such 'Harry' ways broke the ice.

The cot for Fleur was placed at the side of Gavin and Elizabeth's bed in the master bedroom.

'For my little sister,' said Maria, stroking the blanket through one of the sidebars.

'That's right, and when she's grown into a big girl like you we'll have to think of the two of you sharing a room.' Maria looked unimpressed.

'Let's go find Grumps, I wonder what he's getting up to?' Maria was gurgling, riding high on her daddy's shoulders.

'Down daddy! Down!' she squealed as they pushed open again the door into Christopher's room and she ran to pick up her well-loved 'Grumps' teddy bear.

In the first two hours of being home, it was as if they had never been away.

'Come on Annie. Will we leave them be now?' Harry said, attempting to stand up for the umpteenth time.

'I'm just finishing my tea, dear,' answered Annie with one of those looks that put Harry firmly in his place.

'Can I help you unpack, or put the little ones to bed?'

'Maybe tomorrow night, thank you Annie. You go and get some well-earned sleep. You'll be sleeping like a couple of tops tonight. So good to see you and Harry again.'

'Aye! Well come on Harry, I've the meal to put on yet.'

'That's where you're wrong my dear, if I can get a word in edge ways! Your husband is taking you out for a meal to the Rose and Crown tonight; table booked and everything. No arguing, it's my treat for you.'

How Harry enjoyed telling Annie about the surprise treat in front of the doctor and his wife. As they walked up the hill to go back home and change for their evening out they said little to each other; contented with linked arms Harry and Annie walked on.

The whole village seemed aglow with the doctor's return and the little girls were such a joyful focus for everyone; although there always seemed to be a cobweb hanging in the air, one that couldn't easily be blown away in quiet memory of Christopher. You could hear it in the tenderness of the voices towards Maria and Fleur; the doctor knew it and Elizabeth knew it and their hearts remained touched at being home again, with the moon, once more, over their doorstep.

CHAPTER TWO   SILVER LININGS

The sun was streaming through the window as Polly wakened into a gorgeous Sunday.

O, no! She thought, is that the time already?

Polly had arranged to meet her friend Sam at the Mill for a spot of lunch. Sundays without Philip highlighted her grief.

Otterton Mill was somewhere Philip and Polly had frequented; it always cheered them up and they used to go to the folk nights. Polly loved the fact that she continued coming, not feeling out of place whether she was sitting on her own or meeting up with one of her friends. It was a great place to while away some time, maybe have lunch and you could always people watch. As Polly turned into the Mill's car park, her mobile phone was beeping. A text from Sam;

SO SORRY CAN'T MAKE IT CHANGE OF PLAN HOW ABOUT TUESDAY? SAM

Polly replied that Tuesday would be fine. What a shame! 'Never mind,' she thought. She was just deciding to go in and have a coffee anyway when another idea sprang to mind. Three quarters of an hour later Polly found herself pulling in to Exeter St David's for her silver lining treat.
'Day return to Penzance, please.'

Polly enjoyed reading and being fairly quiet. She valued her friends who would call spontaneously, especially now that she was on her own, but it was funny how that so highly valued thing could also just sometimes feel too much.
'Brilliant!' Polly thought to herself as she found a window seat at a table with two seats free. Opposite, a friendly couple looked happily engrossed in Sudoku as well as checking email on their phones. Three hours there, three hours back.

Polly made sure her mobile was switched off and decided that this was her own special time that chance had brought her, an opportunity to have free reading time with the manuscript. No one would be there to interrupt. No one even knew that she was making this journey. 'How fantastic!' She hadn't been to Penzance since she was a child and to have six or seven hours of time to read was a bonus. She was not alone; she was sitting amidst others, so now her own personal journey with the story could begin.

C3: Growing up at Springhill. August 1961

Springhill had a charm of its own. Like the parent to parents, in its 'womb like way' across generations of comings and goings: births, marriages and deaths, Springhill stood firm, strong and was always welcoming even if at times: awesome. Springhill had twenty-four rooms over three floors. Down the steps that lead to the basement and the surgery was a child's paradise. I suppose part of its appeal was that the basement area was so separate from the house; full of different 'clinical' smells and sounds, papers and pens, intercoms, stethoscopes, a buzzing system that would flash up for the next patient to go through from the waiting room: it was magic to Maria and me - another world.

Over the years, stories abounded about things that happened there. The one we particularly liked became known to us as 'the waiting room saga'. The waiting room electric fire used to go on around 2pm in order to warm up for the evening surgery that didn't start until 4pm. 'What a waste,' thought a small group of pensioners who decided to meet there where it was snug and warm and quite private: an ideal venue to practice square dancing. Can you imagine their surprise and the doctor's surprise when they were caught? Tommy was clapping and whistling out a tune as the knees up took place and Dr Brian returned home early and unexpectedly from his visits to the lively commotion that was taking place. O, dear, Tommy couldn't really see what the problem was, though he was described as going rather red in the face when caught.

Miss Wilkinson was one of the receptionists and she used to keep a very tidy office. A pretty person; neat in how she kept her desk, neat in how she dressed, in how she wore her hair and in how she answered the phone in that concerned but slightly detached sort of way. She always wore lovely perfume, a solid stick that she rubbed onto her forehead. We would watch the many different things that would complete her day; we saw her filing notes and messages; feeding pencils into the clamped pencil sharpener as she whizzed the handle around leaving lots of filings in the glass end and very long points on the pencils! She always checked the paper store where the biros, red and black, were tied together in clusters with rubber bands. We never seemed to run out of anything. There was a stamp that you pressed onto a pad of ink for the date and name and address. There was a typewriter, which had a hood over it to keep it neat and tidy. She always placed a tissue like piece of paper behind the main copy with a sheet of carbon paper in between before she rolled these into the typewriter.

'And what is she complaining of?' Miss Wilkinson would ask as she answered the phone.
'How long has she had the pain?' She would look and sound concerned, though perhaps, by the end of the hectic morning surgery, she sounded more concerned than she looked, and she would recite:
'The doctor is out on his rounds at the moment, but I will let him know when he comes in.'

Miss Wilkinson had a tinkling voice with soothing tones and rarely became flustered. She had to deal with the most stressed patients at times and often had us to contend with too, not to mention the doctors who would do their ranting and raving in front of her some times:
'Would you like a cup of coffee, or tea perhaps...one sugar?' She would offer as a panacea, even if it wasn't wanted, the very mention of it seemed to relieve some of the tension. She always knew, their 'roar was worse than their bite.'
It was difficult for me to imagine that Miss Wilkinson had a life outside of Springhill but, of course, she did. I was ten or eleven when she started to refer to her boyfriend as 'my fiancé,' this was my initiation into understanding the meaning of the word and all the planning that would follow. I remember looking at her hands, and admiring her ring, but being much more in awe of her nails. They were beautiful; I

didn't think I had ever seen long nails like that before and they were delicately shining with an 'oyster pink' nail polish that looked so natural. I wondered if all people who became engaged automatically had nails like that.

Down in the surgery Maria and I had so many ailments over those young years. We had headaches, cuts and bruises, tummy aches, sore throats. We would take it in turns as to which one of us was doctor or patient. Once an empty chair became the patient and I was the doctor and Maria became the visiting consultant. She made me laugh until I cried as she took on many of his characteristics. In those days, the GP would call out the specialist to do a domiciliary visit with him to assess the patient for priority admission to hospital, so we were used to those visits happening and seeing the consultants come. One wore a bow tie, another was extremely tall and we used to mimic him stooping so that his head didn't touch the ceiling.

One of us would press the button that flashed the light through in the waiting room, ringing through on the intercom when the next patient was called to see the doctor: it was one of those games that went on and on, becoming more sophisticated, as we got older. The being able to communicate with each other from different rooms added to the fun.
I remember copying the 'whooshing' sound of the bubbling sterilization tray and being allowed to play with fragments from bandages that hadn't been used.

'How's Mrs Gooseberry Barton this morning?'
'Mrs Gooseberry Barton is feeling a little peaky, and I mean, I have had diarrhoea, my tummy is so sore' Maria said as she giggled, remembering to change her words to the first person in order to be in role.
'I thought I had better ring the surgery this morning,' said Maria still amused at the thought of saying a diarrhoea thing!
'I see,' replied 'Dr Fleur' stroking her chin.

'I think a couple of doses of kaolin and morphine might be the best option and a good night's sleep,' intervened a voice that startled us; there we were like rabbits caught in the headlights, by Dr Brian, who had picked up the other phone and heard our play. A bit like the pensioners, with squeals of embarrassment and mouse-like speed, we scampered out of his way. For months afterwards, we were too shy to look him straight in the face having been well and truly caught speaking about 'a bottom' thing!

Above the surgery was a hive of activity too. Mother was a doctor's wife of the old school variety. There was the ritual known as 'elevenses'. This was tea or coffee time when the surgery staff came upstairs into the house for their break, an everyday occurrence; this became a highlight of the school holiday. At 'elevenses', Miss Wilkinson, Mrs Welsh, Annie, and mother would be in the kitchen around the large kitchen table, whilst our father and his partner would be in the study, both having a rest and discussing any cases or business of the day quietly and confidentially. Sometimes we would hear ripples of laughter coming from the study and would have loved to have known what that was all about, but learned that there were things you wouldn't be told or ask about because they were 'Confidential!'

At 'elevenses', you would hear all sorts about Miss Wilkinson's fiancé and the forthcoming wedding, about the families of Mrs Welsh and Annie and they would ask about Maria and me. Mother was a darling and I suppose her childhood of being a vicar's daughter was a natural prelude to being how she was in adulthood. She was just perfect as the doctor's wife and well used to living a dedicated sort of life, with the need to multi task and yet have time for everything. The kitchen and the aga cooker were wonderfully welcoming and quite the hub of the house. Home, family, Harry and Annie, the surgery, music and dancing, village fetes, visits to Sister Bernadette; this was our world, and when I think of

Springhill, I think of it growing up with us, almost like it was a person in its own right.

Half term holidays were often associated with an overnight stay at Annie's; she made such a fuss of us but in a simple way. Even though her Susan and Billy were older than us, we still enjoyed their company. The big attraction for me was Clover and there was so much space and a feeling of being away from the village.

I think my first crush was on Billy. I often wonder if Annie noticed how flustered I would be around him, but his angular body looked so fit as he so willingly chopped logs for the fire and brought the coke in for the park ray. I blush still at how I really had to stop myself from following him around like a lap dog all the time that I was there. He never said much to me but I hung on to every word and heard myself tittering with laughter at the slightest thing. Yes, my eleven-year-old crush was definitely on Billy Lowther.

Visits to the convent

'My, how Maria has grown, just look at all that hair and rosy cheeks; and Miss Fleur, why she looks like an angel, those eyes would melt many a heart.' The nuns at the convent cooed and fussed with complete joy over us, 'the girls' and had made a special tea: ham salad, soft bread and butter (both brown and white) and the most delicious trifle, which was served in individual glasses. Each trifle was decorated with hundreds and thousands and silver little balls that left such a sweet taste in your mouth. I loved visiting the convent, which happened at least twice a year. The journey felt an eternity, but the boiled sweets helped, given to us in measured proportions, and once we saw the sign 'welcome to

Cumbria,' everything started to look different to my eleven-year-old eyes - as if we were in another country.

The convent was tucked away, hidden in a remote corner between Derwent Water, Blencathra and Skiddaw near the small market town of Keswick. In the early evening you could hear the nuns' singing fly though the air in silvery waves of sheer joyfulness. It didn't seem to matter what the words were as their voices uplifted you in a way that made you have to stop for a moment to listen. I often wonder what it was, that held the magic of those visits; was it the ritual of the same things every year, the association of our family journey there, the boiled sweets as children, that became al fresco picnics as we grew older, the peaceful smiles of the nuns, the regular 'surprise' of the colouring books?

Sister Bernadette, who seemed to be a special friend of mother's, had an oval face with a wisp of hair peeping out from under her veil, which framed her face, and there were always a few hairs on her chin. The hair under the veil looked thin and white as if it belonged to someone old, but her face seemed younger. It was a curious thing to me, to think mother and she were such good friends: kindred spirits. Mother told Sister how sad we had all been with the loss of 'nana'. I was never sure whether Sister had known her personally, but I do remember wishing they'd stop talking about her as I was holding back the tears.

There was always a 'cup of tea welcome' in the parlour, which was a highly polished room that some- times made me sneeze. Occasionally, I would need my spray. I would wheeze a bit in some atmospheres and situations. The spray I took was usually kept in mother's bag; it was quite a contraption, something that offered you little discretion and you had to get it going by manually squeezing a black rubber pump.

There was usually a bonus to the visit; some sort of small gift for Maria and I, which would keep us occupied, and this would routinely be a crayoning or tracing book. Then there was a large round Cadbury's Roses tin, which would be lifted from the trolley onto the table and contained every colour and kind of crayon you could imagine. This activity time helped entertain us and keep us quiet whilst our parents spoke with the Sisters.

'Come along this way- now this is where Sister teaches the eight and nine year olds this year.'

Mother explained to Maria and me that Sister Bernadette was a teacher. I really liked her but I just couldn't imagine her being a teacher! For a while I didn't think of her as being a woman (or a man), she was just Sister Bernadette. We had been taken through the chapel, along the corridor where my new shoes had squeaked embarrassingly along the mosaic floor, through to the school - speaking in the third person was something we weren't used to but 'Sister' was smiling at us both, and then at mother, and by the end of our visits we got used to her referring to herself as well as the other 'nuns' as 'Sister'.

'Hello Sister Anne,'

'Hello Dr and Mrs Andrews.'

'What a wonderful job you've done there, thanks be to God,' Sister Anne slightly inclined her head modestly to Sister Bernadette's words; she was wearing a large overall and was busy 'inking' the black-board, in preparation for another year.

'I hoped we could get it looking like brand new again!'

The desks in the classroom were neatly in rows.

'We'll have eighteen in the class this year, twelve girls and six boys.'

'That'll be a lot for you, Sister. You'll need to keep up your strength, now so you will. Let's hope they're a class of little angels for you now.'

'Sister' would never be a Miss Taylor, but having seen her classroom I had a better picture of her standing in front of her class. Even her voice, quiet as it was, had a teacher's ring about it and she definitely had that way of explaining things.

On our visits it was mostly mother and Sister who spoke with each other, with an occasional offering or introduction of some gentle laughter from our father but there was always that point in conversation when faces would specifically turn to Maria and I and expect something back from us.
'What is it dear', mother asked as she saw me quietly shifting weight from one foot to the other and looking a little peaky.
'Wanting to go again?'
Of course I did!

Upon returning to the room I felt an awkward silence, broken by a clearing of the throat from mother (predictably it would not be long before the next phase happened and the expectation would be that Maria and I would give some kind of performance).

Mother told Sister Bernadette about Maria moving up to the big school now and settling in well.
'Maria has such a gift for physical education, and the teacher there has an extremely good rapport with her.'
'Isn't that a wonderful thing, now?'
'It is, and Maria is also extra good at art and is also learning to play the violin.'
'You're a busy young girl'
'Fleur, bless her is to be starting at her big school next year, sings like a little bird you know' added father.
'How beautiful! Will Fleur be giving us a song then?' Sister asked. I swallowed hard.
'You shouldn't have said,' I whispered to my father and I felt my mind blank with nerves, there would be no escaping now!

'Kumbaya, my lord,' mother whispered.
'Come on,' said Maria impatiently.
'Kumbaya my Lord, Kumbaya,
 Kumbaya my Lord, Kumbaya,
 Kumbaya my Lord, Kumbaya'
'O, Lord Kumbaya,' Mother joined in followed by Sister in the last refrain. I carried on singing. I did not look at anyone. Suddenly, there were no more words to sing and a big clap especially from Sister signalled the end.

'That's beautiful dear! What a lovely voice!' she clapped, politely. Mother just smiled. Modesty aside, it was true, singing was something I could do with ease, and it took me ages to understand why, for some people it was hard to hit the right notes. I sang my best when I could really sing out loud and I loved the echo when I was in the bath. With no prompting, Maria knew it was her turn next so we moved two stand chairs away from the wall so that her performance could begin - two or three pirouettes followed which rolled into two double cartwheels, followed by a somersault on the floor and then she came to a standing position with her arms raised high in the air.

'All that energy, you'll be winning medals at the new school!'
Maria was giggling in response to the sisters' praise.

It was on this summer visit that our parents told the nuns of their decision to send Maria and I to separate secondary schools.
'We have given it much thought and think this is a way of letting them'
'Blossom individually' Sister Bernadette finished off mother's sentence.
That was the way it was on these visits: there was always a lot of chatter and news to share!

C4: Our Grandmothers

Nana Hastings, who died when I was eight years old, lived in the village of Wycoller, near Trawden in Lancashire - I loved it there, especially playing by the bridge. Your imagination could really run away with you, both inside and outside of her home. She always seemed very old to me.

I remember Nana telling me that the picture of the girl with the wavy hair blowing in the breeze was herself when she was young. I remember looking at her intently as I tried making the young face fit into the older one but it seemed impossible. I used to snuggle into her bed and watch her lit up only by the small night-light (kept on a saucer which was filled with a little water for safety) as she peeled off layers of corsets. The ritual of undressing seemed to take forever and I was careful not to be seen.

Nan would say some prayers out loud before she went to sleep, but she also told me there were other kinds of prayers, the made-up sorts that we could say to ourselves. My Nana Hastings was very into nature and identifying different birds that came into the garden. We would often walk in the countryside just by her house and across the stream. She had a pace of life that was so very thoughtful and I loved her very much.

Sometimes we would see signs of a family of hedgehogs and we would put a saucer of milk out for them at night, in case they visited us again. She made the best ginger cake in the world; the top of it was dark and shiny, tacky and sticky and she always made it in a roasting tin. Maria and I were allowed to help with it and I don't think there is a recipe in the world that could be as good as Nana Hasting's ginger cake. Then there was the scraping of the bowl at the end. No wonder her baking skills had been so welcome in the vicarage.

On reflection now, I think people lightly amused Nana; she never seemed to worry about anything very much and could relay many a story. The thing was though, you never felt she was laughing 'at,' anyone in particular; she was just bringing a tale to life. She was always extremely concerned to be fair to both Maria and I. We usually visited her together but if ever I went on my own, then I knew Maria would be invited the next time.

Nan Hastings had the most amazing lap to sit upon - it felt warm and safe and she would rock in her chair to and fro. Maybe it wasn't so much her lap, as her knees that were so Nana because, as ungainly and sagging as they were with rolls of wobbly bits on the sides; sitting on her knee remains one of the most memorable experiences of my life. Nana's rocking chair was covered over the winter time with a blanket crocheted in rows of green, brown and orange while in the summer, the chair would be revived and given a new lease of life with nana's handmade 'patchwork quilt chintz,' (which smelt of mothballs) that would be p r o u d l y draped over the chair. These covers both brought an amazing feel to her room and a cosiness to her knee and in a way it was those three things, the covers, that chair and grandma's knee that to me made her home truly 'nana's'.

'There's nothing like a good pot of tea,' she'd say and we were used to drinking it from an early age, and knew how important it was to warm the tea pot and that it should, of course, be poured from a 'china teapot.' Nana's tea tasted special because besides making a good brew she added to it sterilized milk. Nana would let one of us take the top from the bottle with the bottle opener: it would then be poured into the milk jug, up to the three quarters mark, which you judged with your eye. She would tell us repeatedly that our grandpa loved sterilized milk, 'it keeps well, you see, and we didn't always have fridges, you know,' and so she always had a muslin cloth with beads crocheted round it that you put over the jug of milk to keep the flies out.

From the opening sentence of Nana's stories, she had us spell bound! and I would want to know what was going to happen next. There were the sort of stories that we called her 'used to' ones.

'Go on, tell us another 'used to' story about our mummy when she was a little girl.'

The best stories Nana told were the 'David and Wendy' ones. They became our make believe friends and they had all kinds of adventures. Sometimes during the day we might ask about them but with a little smile and a shake of her head she would tell us:

'Later, bedtime,' and we would jig about saying:

'Will you Nana? Promise?'

'You'll have to wait and see,' was the reply, an answer which was sure to whet our appetite and 'better' our behaviour whilst we waited. Nana always made sure we said our prayers at night and 'Wendy and David' followed the prayer time. She and grandpa had always said their evening prayers together.

I remember her when she used to come over to Springhill; it was the way she was simply 'there.' when we came in from school. She would come for the day or sometimes for an overnight stay and was a big help to mom, whether it was doing some ironing or making a couple of apple pies for her.

I remember the day well that mother told us Nana had died. We arrived back from school to see Annie in the kitchen ready with some orange juice and a biscuit - our usual home time welcome, only Annie wasn't usually there on a Wednesday after school, so we both sensed something had happened.

'Are you all right, Annie?'

'I'm fine dear,' she gave me a big squeeze. In the study I saw our father putting his arm up affectionately as he spoke quietly to someone on the phone and as the call ended I heard the tail end of a sentence, '...speak to the children.' Within minutes, two little girls heard the sad news of their Nana's passing; she had died in her sleep from a heart attack. Mother had been trying to ring her but when there had been no reply for the third time she went over to the house and so faced the shock of having to use her key to let herself in, only to find her worst fears confirmed. For weeks, months and years I missed Nana Hastings very, very much.

Our other grandmother lived over the hill in Yorkshire; she liked to be called Grandma Lillian and she lived just on the outskirts of Clapham. She used to speak of her 'salad days' and for ages she was 'Green Grandma' in my mind. I often thought in colours regarding days of the week and months of the year: Monday was turquoise, Thursday - always purple; Saturday was silver so naturally a grandma with 'salad days' would have to be 'green'.

Grandma Lillian had a room full of books and Maria and I would walk in quietly and handle the books with great care as if they might break if mistreated. Grandma loved to read and certainly encouraged Maria and me with our reading, writing and learning. Books were very special things in her eyes, 'beyond price,' and we came to love reading slowly and surely; perhaps I think I was a little more into them than Maria, maybe because in some ways I was turning out to be more of an indoor person than Maria, who spent every possible moment outside. I loved the smell and feel of the books at grandma's and the way we all were comfortable being quiet in each other's company when we picked one up to read.

On a Saturday we would take the black shopping bag from under the stairs and go to the library at Settle. The children's library was bright and cheerful, and Miss Baines would say to me:

'Good morning and how is Miss Fleur today? What can we get you today? A nature book, an adventure, or is it to be something about the past. A history book perhaps?'
Have a look on the squirrel table – we've arranged a selection of books on it just this morning, ideal for someone your age, or maybe a little bit older.'

I loved the squirrel table: it was rectangular in shape, and an ideal height for children to reach a book from. The legs were carved in the shape of a squirrel; I wonder what's happened to all those Saturday morning children who used to choose their books from the same place as me?

Grandma Lillian played the piano. Her favourite piece was: the Moonlight Sonata. I would watch her fingers move over the keys, so fast, and see the movement of her hands undulate with the expression and tone of the sounds and her face would change as the notes changed and sounded different. I felt so proud of her. 'I would never be able to play like that,' I thought, and I was right. Play I couldn't do, but the capacity to hear and love music is a wonderful thing, filling in so many corners in life and that I could do.

To my little girl's ears, grandma sounded just a little bit posh and on the phone she sounded even more posh. She was always very polite and had her own distinctive style of doing things and always tried to show us that her way was 'best.' She was a complete darling to us when we lost our 'nana,' and was always rather sad that we never knew our dear grandfather who had died when Maria was three and before we had ever come to England: he had suffered shellshock in the war. I used to like her showing us his photograph where he had his arms wrapped around a little boy who was holding a rabbit. We used to hear that it was 'Snowy' the rabbit and the little boy was our brother Christopher. I could see the likeness to my father and to Maria in Christopher, and it was good to see a photograph of our grandfather whom we had never known.

Maria and I visited our Grandma Lillian regularly and she would also invite both of us separately to stay during the holidays and we both loved that separate time as well as going there together. Grandma Andrews had become a nurse when she was in her early 30s and was very dedicated to her work. She loved purple and combing our hair into styles tied with a ribbon. She would tell us often how good it must be to have little girls and then she would tell us about our father when he was a little boy. Her stories were more 'so you see stories' or, 'the moral of that story is'.

'Your daddy was a very clever boy, but he was never one for going up for prizes, so could have worked harder ('so you see', we thought to ourselves) he'll have great hopes for you two girls to do even better than he did.'

Grandma died when I was eleven years old. I remember walking quietly into her house, and hearing the clocks that were still tick, tick, ticking, away. She had six clocks of different kinds: a grandmother, granddaughter and a long case wall clock as well as a Westmorland chime mantle clock and two other carriage clocks. 'How sad!' she wouldn't be there anymore to wind them.

Neither of us went to the funeral; we stayed at home. We wept, we wept bitterly.

Now, with both our grandmothers gone, would life ever be the same again? For a while I found it hard making conversation with our parents. They looked sad and worn out from all the sorting out that there was to do. Mother was not very well around that time so Annie used to stay with us sometimes.

There are still moments in my life when I hear a piece of music particularly 'The Moonlight Sonata.' and in the same moment it's as if I can hear her clock ticking again, in a way that can bring tears to my eyes and a lump in my throat and then there are other times when humming around in my head the same sort of things, the same notes simply bring happy sounds of a nostalgia that leaves a warmth, as cosy as Nana Hastings's crochet blanket.

C5: SEPTEMBER 1963.

Monday morning came, the start of my first day at the big school. I was so excited, so scared, so happy!
I felt like a 'little girl' again; flat and shapeless compared to the big girls in the top class and yet it wasn't a minute since I had been in the top class towering above the little ones at my old school, all of five weeks ago.

Annie came to see me dressed up for school and to wave me off. I absolutely loved her and it was always good to see her out of the pinafore apron that wrapped around her curves and with her sandy 'pepper an' salt' hair, freshly groomed into a neat little bun at the nape of her neck, instead of the more familiar tousled look from the steam of cooking.
'Now you have a good time! With all that learning you look a proper 'bobby dazzler,' in your uniform. I love that colour of brown!'

I can still remember that moment when she gave me a kiss and I smelt the cologne she had put on, especially for me (or maybe it was for her Harry who had driven her over).
'Hurry along darling, we don't want you late for your first morning do we?' mother called, adding, 'see you later Annie, so sweet of you to have come.'

'I don't want to go,' all of a sudden, my tummy was heaving with all the excitement that had been building up over the last few months; I felt in a dizzy sweat of panic and my new shoes were feeling awfully tight.
'Come on,' said my father as he hooted the horn but he had already stepped from the car, opening the door, arm around me, to bundle me into the back seat.
'No time, for nervousitis, you'll soon be just fine you'll see.'
His voice was warm, firm and reassuring, and his made up words always helped. Reluctantly I knew he would be right, I'd be just fine.

'Daddy's right, Fleur, you'll be coming home tonight full of...'
'Beans,' added father and, true enough, I did have a lot to tell them, but that morning somehow seemed to set a pattern in me for future Monday mornings.

I remembered the explanation to Sister Bernadette as to why we were to be sent to two separate schools, but that first morning, I would have given anything to have seen my sister at break time in the playground. Maria was well settled in her big school by the time I started mine. Most of her friends had expected me to go to the same school, after all, their sisters did and I always had difficulty explaining it myself, as it was one of those parental decisions that you just had to agree with. On the other hand we would often have tales to tell each other from the day, so somehow we got by with it.

Maria and I both had a few outside of school things to do; extra lessons in music and ballet and, just occasionally, we would end up in the same concert. I remember loving that and always looking up to my big sister. Sometimes, I thought Maria really wanted to highlight our differences, whilst I was always pleased when folk said how alike we were! One thing was certain; I always knew she would look out for me.

Mr Pickles, the piano teacher, used to come to our house to give me my fortnightly lesson and mother would routinely bring him tea with two rich tea biscuits (half way through the lesson) served in the blue willow pattern cup, saucer and plate with matching teapot. Maria was also very busy with team sports for the school. She did brilliantly and she had an abundance of energy. There was a lovely openness about her and she had a smile that knocked you for six. I used to think if she were at my school I would have loved her to be the head girl.

Revisiting one's childhood, as we all do, is like referring to a well-worn reference book. The words still remain the same; but somehow, they are capable of being transformed into new meanings previously hidden to our understanding, as we ourselves move through life. I suppose, when I look back to those days at Springhill, I can see that it offered a rare form of eclipsed security and yet this could prove in some ways to be both a positive and a negative in my later life. It would be unusual to expect to easily repeat those feelings of security from the world of Springhill and all that came with it - **the moon above us, which often seemed to be directly over our front door at night.**

I am sure the war had left its mark in giving parents of our generation a depth of perspective of seeing beyond petty things that some people might worry about. For our family there was also the loss of our brother Christopher. He was always there, an invisible presence that felt spooky at times. Maria and I had never known him; our mother and father rarely spoke of him but he was there. There were the silences that tensed up around things that made me want a brave conversation but then other things happened or the phone rang and the bubble was gone. I am sure we all had moments of thinking how good it would have been to have a brother around the place to offer that other sort of perspective and love. He was always ahead of Maria somehow, in people's minds. Even when people asked how old Maria was they would sometimes say, 'really, how time flies,' as if to stop short of, 'so long since Christopher passed away.'

Whatever was happening at home, the practice would still be there on our doorstep, so there was little chance to get true breaks, especially for our parents. Patients would come to the house, sometimes out of hours in distress and mother would hold the fort and give some help to them whilst father politely told them he was not on call and tried to redirect them. Behind closed doors some of these intrusions became a pressure; mother seemed almost to welcome them, perhaps it would have been very reminiscent of her home at the vicarage but Springhill wasn't a vicarage and the boundary for our father had to be different. He was dedicated too but sometimes tired of the endless need to get it right medically, psychologically and socially for his patients. We needed to live simply as a family and in many ways (irrespective of the hive of activity that was home) we did succeed in such fun family times and always had parents, family and friends we could turn to. The idea that there was always 'someone worse off than you' was quite a theme in our family. True as it is, sometimes thinking like this can stop you from speaking up about something you're having difficulty with, because you feel guilty for bringing it up.

Spring to summer 1966; a wall of adolescence started just for a while to make the difference in Maria's and my ages seem bigger. Maybe it was the lack of conflict we had experienced as a family up to that point which made Maria's adolescence stand out all the more, hitting us like an unearthly hurricane. Whatever or however we tried to look at it, her behaviour had switched from green light to blaring red! Suddenly, as if overnight, the little village of Pen-y-dale seemed too claustrophobic to her. Everything around her was 'boring' and the bright lights of London seemed a million light years away. Gymnastics and athletics no longer held an interest for her and were replaced by teeming hormones and a desire bursting through her for alternative interests and excitement. Pen-y-dale, walking the hills and riding, were no longer Maria's 'dubonnet and bitter lemon!'

School rang up with a few problems; Maria with teachers and pupils, Maria and homework, Maria and being late. On one or two occasions, Maria had been reported missing from school only to be spotted hanging around the bus station in the next town. What was happening to her? Mother and father would go to school and then for a little time things would seem to settle down. I do remember hearing that if she carried on as she was doing she might be expelled which, at the time, seemed like the end of the world. I remember hearing mother reasoning with the teachers and then I would hear her reasoning from another point of view with Maria. Even when Maria was at her most rude, mother's style was to explain it away – she was the eternal peacemaker. Maria, for a while, saw everything as being someone else's fault. Perhaps we should have been prepared to see she might have been right at least sometimes. Instead everything was seen through the lens of 'she's just being difficult.'

'You're always going on at me. Me, me, me, all the time, just because I don't want to be a saint like you,' she would shout, staring at mother, 'I didn't get my first lipstick until I was seventeen' (she would mimic mother's voice in an exaggerated way). 'Why should I care if you didn't get one till you were seventeen, so what if I've worn it since I was fifteen? And before you say it, Grandma Lillian wouldn't be 'turning in her grave,' or Nana Hastings, for that matter, they were both more *with it* than you!' The prolonged 'OO' from the 'you' sounded like finger wagging at poor mother. At this moment, I would think, 'if only Maria would be more cooperative. Where's father?'

Mother is carrying on stoically, patiently trying to listen, yet I notice how there's something that Maria seems to feel as overbearing about the way she is handling things. It's not helping Maria and in a different way neither am I. Mother thinks she can see others' points of view but has a self-righteousness about her that makes it very difficult really. I can see how worn out she feels from Maria's relentlessly attacking behaviour so much so that she has had to switch off a bit.

I am feeling claustrophobic; I can smell the polish and my chest feels tight. Springhill, such a haven, has a downside too. It is special, unique, magnetic, central to the community, but we are not free to come and go. We are in service, we are framed; we are as much propped up by the negatives rather than the privileges other people see. 'Home,' our real home truly is a warm and loving bedrock of support to us but it is scary growing up because the steps outside are big ones to take and it feels like there's less room to practice, as many people watch us.

Poor Maria!

Up until that point, I hadn't really appreciated the significance of Maria being the first of us to leave home. Suddenly, I see Maria's wings as the wings of a second phase fledgling. A baby bird makes several attempts to fly but unlike the baby bird who has all the encouragement from its parents, in this second phase of flying the struggle is bigger and the growing baby is responding to her own experience of the world around her which feels a bit different from her parents. Instead of supports, everything feels like an obstacle course and because we are at Springhill, we are more noticeable to everyone.

Father is looking exasperated - the volume is turning up again.

'I think you owe your mother an apology, can't you see you have upset her?'

'I'm all right dear,' mother says through her tears with a faint smile of relief that he is there beside her.

'We are trying to understand you darling. It isn't easy growing up and sometimes people can be a bit jealous of you. You know what I mean, darling?' Mother was searching for some gentle response from Maria.

'Well you're not making a very good job of understanding me are you? I'm just about completely the opposite of you - I'm just like my father.'

'I was only telling Annie the other day, sometimes I worry for you Maria, that you might be going a little deaf. Your

Grandma Lillian did start to you know, very young in life, when she was about your age I think'

'Going deaf? What are you on about? What were you talking to Annie about me for, anyway?'

Silence fell.

'How ridiculous', Maria thought, and so did I. I didn't say anything but was thinking: she's just 'growing up!'

'What would Christopher have been like? What kind of son and brother would he have been? What difference would his kind of humour have made to us all? What would his male-ness have brought?'

'If only,' - two of the biggest words, that kept me stuck in a uselessly ' in between' stance. If only I wasn't so 'wishy – washy' I could have spoken up for Maria. If only Christopher had been around, Maria wouldn't perhaps have been strug-gling as much to lead the way.

At Angela's house I started to notice life just seemed so much less complicated. Angela's mum loved dressmaking; she had never been taught but had found a way that brought some good results. Occasionally she tried to make something and it was a bit of a flop or she'd pin something on us and then ask us to help with bits of the hem, which sometimes then ended up being slightly lopsided, but it was such a light hearted way to learn and it didn't seem to matter so much how things turned out because you could always turn it into something else. We were similar sizes and shapes, so Angela and I could swap clothes and play at making things look dif-ferent. It was so refreshing to have things, non- people things to think about. I realized one evening when I was there at Angela's that the phone only went once instead of being a continuous hot line like it was at home. Angela was well loved too but there was something about it that reminded me of Nana Hastings and how she did things.

Angela's dad would really shout and bawl at her sometimes and most of the time, she gave as good as she got. She was sometimes further rebuked for that, but it was over sooner than it would have been at home. Perhaps that was as much to do with their telephone not ringing all the time. We forever had conversations interrupted so you then had to get back to what you were saying, so things were less likely to blow over quickly as they did at Angela's house.

Angela's sister Carolyn seemed so grown up: she was nearly four years older than us and had a very handsome boyfriend, James. Carolyn always seemed to dress in the latest fashion and she started to blossom as she piled on the weight. Eventually she told us she was pregnant. Mr and Mrs Wilkinson were shocked and embarrassed. They clearly didn't like it but quickly helped to arrange a small registry office wedding and Angela bought herself a peach coloured bridesmaid dress. Carolyn and James stayed for a year in the family home with baby Tim until they got a council house of their own. Staying over at each other's houses was such a good thing for Angela and me to do. Not that either of us would really have wanted to swap permanently but at least it gave us another perspective on things.

When Angela stayed with us her dad would warn her not to come home from Springhill, with 'high and mighty ideas about things!' She never did. She loved coming to stay and it was usually late at night that she would pretend what it would have been like if she'd been born my sister.

'I'd have loved having Camay soap and helping your mother to set the table in the morning ready for the evening meal. And as for your dad, he's gorgeous,' Angela carried on swooning.

C6: Little Women

Around this time, I wanted to support Maria and wanted it all to stop but I suppose I didn't really think there was anything I could do to help without going against our weary parents. Taking chances and risks did not come much into my head. I was just almost too understandingly disposed in the way both our parents were, seeing every view under the sun. I saw conflict as negative. I found it hard to see why some people got so steamed up about their particular belief about something. I used to watch people as they argued, their faces squiggling with stressed voices rising; what was so good about it? Did it achieve anything? I still believe so many people argue pointlessly, when there is often a peaceful way of sorting something out. I realise that the net effect of all of this was that sometimes it must have looked to others as if I hardly existed.

'You make me sick, why do you have to be such an angel? Can't you ever do anything wrong? Go on say something back...don't just stare at me like that...and please don't go running to mummy,'
'Maria, don't speak to your sister like that.'
'Maria, Maria, Maria, Maria, Maria don't you.... Maria this, Maria that.'
That was the 'too much' moment that brought father immediately back into the frame.
'What in Heaven's name is going on?' For one of the first times in my young life I saw our father firing on all cylinders.
'We're just having a fall out,' Maria said defensively.
'That's what you think, I haven't said anything!'
'I haven't done anything either,' continued Maria mimicking a softly spoken whine which aped my voice remarkably.
'That's enough; I WILL NOT have this kind of thing in our home. Whatever has got into you needs sorting out. Go to your room immediately.'

'Go to your …' Maria started her answering back routine but the unusually disapproving look on our father's face stopped her short and she went upstairs. Maria absolutely adored our father and the thought of her having brought this upon herself and seeing his distress made her start to see the need to stop.

Downstairs the dulled tones of parents attempted to rationalise Maria's behaviour, so after a break from dealing with telephone calls, the subject matter reverted back onto the 'what to do with Maria' issue. Swiftly our father broke the next silence with;

'I have been thinking. Maybe we need help.'

'See if I care.' The last thing Maria wanted to see was a shrink.

'Maria,' by this time mother was crying and Maria had run down the stairs, opened the door and slammed it as she walked out in a storming temper into the early evening air.

'Get lost, the lot of you!'

'Is that Maria?' asked a calm voice.

'Will I be glad to get away,' Maria continued her muttering hardly noticing Maureen Smith, who was passing by.

'Is that Maria?' Maria mimicked back

'No, I'm not Maria,' she looked at Maureen full in the face. 'I'm Princess Anne. Of course you know who I am. Why does everyone have to be so polite around here?'

'O, dear', father said as he drew the curtains, as if trying to bring a degree of closure on the scene.

'How rude. Poor Maureen'

'What was that about Princess Anne?' asked mother.

'Maybe you're right and she does need to see a psychiatrist.'

'What's Maureen done wrong?'

'O nothing dear, nothing at all, Maria's just lost her rag and Maureen's caught for it. I didn't say she needed to see someone I said **we** need to see someone. Perhaps we all need to see someone as a family. Don't you think so?

'Family therapy' they call it. Why should Maria have to vent up for all of us and perhaps there are things we should talk to the girls about.'
'Where have I gone wrong?'
'Never said you had, there's no need for us to point the finger at any one thing. Just think about it dear, there are probably a whole lot of things that we could do to sit down and talk about as a family with someone
'Well, I know what you mean, I do try to understand.'

'That's just it; we just need to get off Maria's case and let her grow up.' I had never heard my father sound so revved up, though the point he was trying to make was lost in their pattern of his loving response to mother's emotional self-blame.
'I suppose, it's a long time since we were horrible to our parents, we've forgotten all about it or should I say it's a long time since I was as horrible to my parents... I'm sure you were always a sweetie,' he looked at mother affectionately at her lovely but weary face.
'O, that blasted phone...what can it be now?'

'Hello, can I help you?' Mother's voice was now calm again, the person there to help solve other people's problems not to have them herself, on her own doorstep.
'If we don't hear from her soon, do you think we should ring the police?'

'Fleur, don't you start complicating things.' Mother's words echoed in my ears. I was quietly screaming.

Two hours later, Billy Lowther arrived at the door absolutely drenched and with a protective arm around Maria.
'Just happened to see your Maria, good job too as she'd forgotten her purse and with her having no money on her and it being such a wet night, good job we bumped into each other with me walking the dog, so I thought I'd just leave her home safe.'

Bring Down the Moon

CHAPTER THREE   NEXT STOP PENZANCE.

'Goodness!' Polly looked up, a bit disorientated from her reading.
'Is that the time already? In three quarters of an hour we'll be there!' That was something Polly often did these days, had little conversations in her head. She put her manuscript into her shoulder bag and went to get herself a sandwich. Her mind was absorbing the story. She was enjoying reading about the two girls. An only child herself she had always liked the idea of having a sister.

Polly wondered what Penzance would be like. The last time she had been there was forty-five years ago with her grand-dad Burt - he had brought her there, for a Bank holiday weekend treat. They had travelled by train though, of course in those days, the journey had taken much longer.
'All those years ago', she said to herself, a tear in her eye as she walked along the cobbled street and thought of the 'little Polly' buying cough candy at the tobacconist shop on the corner and remembered how she had chosen a small doll in Cornish costume to give to her mother at the end of the weekend's holiday.

Granddad was such a jolly man, Polly recalled, and they had a very close relationship. He had come to live with her mother and father when Polly was about seven and had the box room upstairs as his bedroom. Polly's parents were very wrapped up in their own lives as their grocery business meant early starts and late closing hours, so Polly learned to occupy herself from an early age. Polly could re-member hearing her granddad's greeting when she came home from school:
'That you love, Polly, is that you? Wait a minute I'm just coming down. I'm just finishing what I'm doing!'
She remembered his distinctive shuffle, a slight limp, his rough cheek brushing on hers as he gave her a raspberry kiss and chuckled, but most of all she couldn't think of him

without remembering his smell; twist tobacco. Lighting his pipe and puffing away was who granddad was. Polly remembered the pipe cleaners and the tapping that he did onto the ashtray, the rolling of the tobacco and the way that thinking and speaking seemed to go with the puffing. A lot of the time he lived in his little room at the top of the stairs and read, but when she was home they were company for each other. 'No trouble, are we? You and me eh? No trouble at all.'

'Here on holiday?' The young waitress said to Polly with a distinctive Cornish burr.
'Just visiting these parts?'
Polly bought herself a fish and chip meal, a pot of tea and some bread and butter. It was delicious - an ideal thing to have somewhere like Penzance. She knew she would return again someday; this would be a 'home' place for the rest of her life. The trick of light from the sea was superb and transformed the colour washed cottages.

5.20pm and Polly managed to find a window seat again. She took out her book, wondering what Maria was getting up to; she liked her plucky spirit and imagined they really got on, as sisters. She was a bit less certain about how the character of Fleur was going to develop. She couldn't put her finger on it but there was something sad about her, and at present she was just a bit too 'goody two shoes,' for her own good. Then Polly found herself worrying about what she'd have to do with it all when she'd finished reading.
'Stop it! Polly', she heard her inner voice tell her, 'stop looking ahead, stay in the ' now' enjoy the story, enjoy your journey.'

'Hurry up Maria. Come on we don't want to miss that train do we?'

It was a wrench waving bye-bye to her at the station. Mother and father had decided to take her by train to see her safely settled and for the first term she would have 'live-in' accommodation in the hospital.

'It'll be the making of her,' mother said with confidence and father agreed.

Life at home at first felt strange without Maria. I really missed her but in some ways I was having my own growth spurt now into womanhood. I enjoyed the sixth form and some of the privileges that came with it. My main subject interests were English, Art and History. I was not sure what I wanted to do on leaving school but I knew what I didn't want, and that was to be a teacher.

Christmas was always brilliant at home and the first Christmas of Maria's return was really something to look forward to. By then even Wanda seemed to know Maria was coming home; she paced up and down by the fire, rolling over, ears pricked up. How she must have missed the 'stroking' attention Maria always gave her!

20th December: 7.0pm.
Maria was home. She walked in looking so elegant with her new 'French pleat' hairstyle, and the blue winter coat of her uniform. There was no doubt about it, her 'new life suited her.

Maria had so much to tell us. She told us about her friends, her room and how she had been 'doing it up.' She told us about the lectures she went to and then, with some amusement, she described 'Matron'; making us laugh so much with her Carry On films! 'plumb' in her voice. On a serious note, I think she was somewhat in awe of the Matron, though she also seemed to be really enjoying working on the wards and interacting with the patients as well.

Maria's room at home had remained exactly as she had left it, so that she could have that undisturbed feeling when she came home.

'Maria' I sang her name quietly.

'Wakey, wakey…' My voice trailed off, when I realized on pushing open the door into her bedroom, that instead of her being sound asleep in bed, Maria was already up.

'Wow, you're up already!'

'Well, never mind…I suppose I'm used to time schedules round the clock these days, so:

O, thanks Fleur, you've beaten me to it, I was just about to make you some tea.

Have you remembered?'

' No sugar for Maria these days.'

'Ah, thanks you have. 'Home' tea tastes best of all!'

'I wanted you to show me how to make a bed properly, you know with hospital bed corners?'

'Well, that's OK I'll just re-make it for you, as ' a demonstration' for your training purposes. Very good, Nurse Fleur, are you ready?

Make sure there is about the same amount of material (sheet) hanging over the mattress at the foot of the bed.

Tuck the bottom of the sheet under the mattress.

Grasp the corner formed by the overlapping fabric with the hand closest to the bed,' and so it went on becoming more and more of a game between us.

'Tell you what Maria, I could see you becoming a Matron one day, Miss Bossy knickers!'

'Now, that could be better,' Maria played along with the Matron suggestion and we both fell about laughing. Had things changed that much since the surgery and 'Mrs Gooseberry Barton' days?'

'It's great to be back home.'

The age gap between us seemed in some ways to have narrowed, although Maria probably thought how naive I was, so

I was aware that she restricted what she was talking to me about on that first visit home, at least where boyfriends were concerned.

'When you're ready, you'll have to come and stay with me in London and hit the highlights.'
I remember thinking that this was a great idea but impossible because of the restrictions of her accommodation. It took me a few more years of growing up and life's experiences to realise that some rules could be a bit more elastic than I had thought. When I did brave it, I was amused by how much Maria let her hair down and yet she could still be sophisticated and remained principled. I was all of a sudden growing up too.

I always loved the peace of the library and the smell of polish as you went in through the big door. I loved the fact that there was a 'Sh' about it that applied to everyone as an unspoken rule. I was always drawn to the nature books. What an amazing thing! All these authors so inspired and putting so much time and thought into writing and finding out about things- for others to simply pick up and read. There was so much to learn from books.

Mr Holmes, the librarian was a wealth of information; he seemed to know every book that had ever found its way into the library and there were also two women who worked alongside him. Miss Thompson worked on reception stamping books and then there was the other older woman: Mrs Thornton. I was never sure whether Miss Thompson and Mrs Thornton got on, but being in a library there was no need to argue or raise your voice, so that would be of little importance.

Mrs Thornton had large pendulous breasts that hung down to her waist, which I think she was quite proud of and with arms folded she would gather them in, as she tried to be helpful to the library users. One Summer I had taken and passed my school exams and was wondering what to do.

As I walked into the library, Mr Holmes approached me with the offer of a job. My answer was long winded as I tried to disguise the fact that I was momentarily overwhelmed by the unexpected offer. I gulped. I kept muttering some kind of 'think about it' response whilst Mr Holmes sort of listened, head to one side but then he intervened, impatiently, with:

'Excuse me I think my dear, someone over there needs me, it's just that it may be a good little job, for you. Why not just give it a try? Our Mrs Thompson is leaving, you see, so if you are interested you need to come in, starting the week after you leave school and sit with her, do some stamping and learn from watching what she does. She will show you how to file the books and keep our records straight. She will help you learn about the different subject areas and what there is stored in different ways other than in reference books. If you want it, the job is yours. I have known you and your family for years so no need for us to have lengthy interviews.' That was just the comment I needed, 'give it a try.'
Thinking of it like that just made all my anxiety disappear. That's all I had to do. I remember running up the lane from the bus that night to tell mother and father and to ring my friend Clare.

Two weeks later, I was working at the library, and had soon successfully completed the initiation period. I moved into one of the bigger attic bedrooms at home, and we had fun decorating it and turning it into more of a bedsit. Suddenly, I felt more grown up and those changes helped make all the difference.

Training to be a librarian was a dedicated thing to do and, in a way, it was a bit like being a teacher: in terms of facilitating a knowledge process but there the similarity ended as far as I was concerned. On reflection, it was a funny thing the way I had all the confidence in the world to perform, to stand up and sing, dance or recite poetry in front of any size of audience and yet, the thought of standing up in front of a sea of school children all looking at me was enough to freak me out!

I always loved the peace of the library and gradually got to know people who came in regularly. I remember Mrs Brown, who lived up the hill by the corner shop. She used to come in to the library once a week. Mrs Brown had lived in the same village and in the same house all her life and yet she told me she had travelled the world in books. I was on a big learning curve in many ways and I found that time passed quickly; there was always plenty to do. It was very exciting when they introduced microfiche: such a brilliant invention and something we all had to learn about together. I seemed to get the hang of it more quickly than some of the more mature librarians.

Allan from the bank was my first serious boyfriend. He was four years older than me, and was always tinkering with cars, whether it was building or repairing them. He had a white-collar job during the day and the overalls came out at night. When he came out with me, he used to like wearing polo neck sweaters, and old spice aftershave. Our courting days over two years consisted of Saturday afternoons at football matches, Sunday evenings at the jazz club, and hours and hours of 'snogging!' Looking back, I can't remember what happened that made Allan 'history.' I think it may have been the result of idle chatter with friends where the word 'boring' often crept into conversation. I didn't really think of him like that but Emma, my friend probably did and what she said mattered to me at the time. He used to drop hints to me about making me Mrs Hargreaves and then he would laugh nervously as if he really knew it would never happen. I do remember feeling the loss of him and his family and to this day I remember him as such a dear person and hope he recalls me fondly too.

C7: The key to the door: 1973.

A dance had been arranged to celebrate my coming of age at the village hall for many of my friends from school days and from work and Maria and I really enjoyed spending time planning things together over the phone. We had all gone to London for Maria's occasion and that had felt absolutely fantastic, especially with her working there, so now we both looked forward to doing it the other way around and Maria and her friends coming north.

I had a new dress made for me. It was my first full-length dress, white with some pale blue detail. There were a few sequins on the front and shoestring straps. It had a sweetheart neckline that fell into a charming low cut detail at the back of the dress, which came as a surprise when you turned around and was both demure and maybe a little bit daring. I remember feeling 'grown up,' maybe something to do with the ' key to that door!' What a chance to catch up with friends who I hadn't seen for ages. We had a girls' night in, six or seven of us before the party and this helped a lot the following morning as we set up the village hall.

'Wow! Fleur, I've never seen you with your hair like that; you must have been hours at Martello's.'
'O, thanks Angela, I suppose it's grown a lot since I saw you last; no, it's not a Martello's job, it's Tina, Maria's roommate from first year. She's so good with clips and hairspray and it always goes a bit wispy when it's long. I didn't know that Maria and Bobby had been cooking up this plan for me and it was Tina's idea to weave the rosebuds in.'
'Perfect! If you have any photographs, please would you let mum have one?'

'Of course!'
'And by the way, she sends you her love and told me to tell you, you're always welcome for those bacon sandwiches.'
Dear Angela, I'd only seen her for two minutes and it was like we'd never been parted.

'Fleur,' Simon was clearing his throat.
'Go on, Simon' Angela encouraged,
'Well, we've some news, we're engaged.'

That was great news, and Simon was much as I had imagined from Angela's tall, dark and handsome description. More hugs followed in fact it was amazing how the talk of weddings, engagements, twenty-firsts, graduation, and flat sharing filled the evening into the early hours of the morning. There were forty-six people at our party. How we didn't burst our eardrums with the music on full blast, I'll never know and we still managed to talk to each other too.

As the evening went on, we sang louder and louder as we swayed in drunken unison to: 'In the jungle, the mighty jungle, the lion sleeps tonight.'

Maria was a gem that night, she never tired of introducing me to more of the London crowd and of course her Keith was there. It would have felt good for me to have a boyfriend then, but it didn't matter. It was the same for Mel and Sophie - they had just recently split up from boyfriends too, so I wasn't alone that way and besides, there was a fair bit of 'talent' at the party. During the evening Jeremy, who had come with Maria's party, came over and asked me to dance. I had noticed him earlier; I didn't know a thing about him but thought he was gorgeous so when I felt his warm hand on my back, I was a quiver.
'Of course, I'd love to dance.'

I honestly can't remember what we talked about but I remember thinking 'is this cloud nine?' I didn't dance with him all night but we had the all-important last waltz together, which ended with a lingering kiss.

The following day everyone was invited to Springhill for a light lunch before going separate ways. Mother and father made quite a fuss of Keith, Maria's boyfriend, who was going to be an accountant and worked in London. I remember feeling a little shy, very conscious of 'last night's kiss.' Would it have meant the same to Jeremy? My confidence however was soon restored the moment our eyes met.

Following the party weekend, Annie came over to help clear up and to have some supper with us. She loved to hear our stories. She brought with her an old photograph album and we had some fun looking back through the photos.

Typical of our house, the phone rang several times that evening, and at twenty minutes past nine, father came in from the study.

'There's someone on the phone wanting to speak to you, Fleur? I thought you'd prefer to be out? Hope I did the right thing in putting him off. I think he said he was called Jeremy?'

'O! Dad, you didn't, did you?'

I was quickly deducing from the twinkle in my father's eye as he spoke, that Jeremy was still dangling on the phone; with that I brushed passed him, pulling a face, yanking the phone from him:

'Hello,' I heard Jeremy's voice and failed in trying to disguise my absolute excitement.

The telephone became our hot line of communication; we longed to speak to each other all the time and our relationship blossomed. I thought he was wonderful and apparently he was smitten by me. Maria seemed very happy for us. Jeremy was in his final year, so we saved every penny we could so that we could fund meeting each other regularly.

The next time we met Maria, she was upset: she had become full of self-doubt, wondering whether nursing was the right thing for her. Keith had finished with her and thought they should 'just be friends' two days before her finals.

'Imagine! Just two days before my finals. Thanks a bunch Keith! Pretty good timing I don't think.' During this time

Maria was glad to have some support from Jeremy. On one occasion his brother came to the hospital and Maria overheard them arguing, she thought this was quite amusing and liked the look of Alistair. She had heard about him before and was glad to be meeting him after all this time. A month later and Maria and Alistair were 'courting.'
'Two brothers with two sisters', Maria laughed at the thought.

Meanwhile back at the library, I continued to learn and to love it, though at the same time I started to feel that I would like to spread my wings and leave one day, but what a wrench it would be to leave all that was home, the family, familiar faces and places, the hills. They were busy days and we had the gaps of time apart to cope with. Jeremy loved running and although I had never been athletic I started to enjoy going to 'keep fit' at the gym and would go for short jogs as part of my new lease of life. I started to love the outdoor air and that exhilarating feeling running gave me... I knew I would never be a marathon runner, but that didn't matter a jot.

I knew with Jeremy at my side, life was full of possibilities.

July 28th 1974
The end of term dance was taking place in London, and Jeremy invited me to come. It was on arriving in London that we learned the news of the engagement of Maria to Alistair. Her ring was a central square sapphire with three small diamonds either side. It suited her hand perfectly and I thought it was gorgeous.
Although the two brothers were not overly alike, you could nevertheless see some similarities between them and I could immediately see what Maria saw in him. 'He'd make a fine barrister one day.' I thought. He certainly knew how to argue his corner. Engaged to my sister, I immediately felt fond of him and I was so excited about the evening ball.

Jeremy and Alistair kept quite separate during the night. The music struck up and we danced in loose ballroom style. As the next dance started, everyone moved to separate spaces, waving arms and 'twisting the night away'. In the distance I saw Alistair start to walk across to me. I looked across at Jeremy when Alistair asked me to dance and I thoroughly enjoyed it thinking what a good dancer he was. As the next number started, Jeremy came over, firmly taking hold of my hand for the next dance. I felt so happy and was already thinking of later that night.

'You have no idea how much I love being with you, every minute,' Jeremy whispered.

I know, it almost hurts sometimes' I whispered back.

That night as we danced and chatted to people I felt we were very much a couple. We came closer and closer, becoming entwined as we danced, the heat was on and my mind was engorged with love for him. Dreamily, I opened my eyes and over Jeremy's shoulder I saw Alistair in the distance looking towards me. 'Engaged to my sister,' I thought, 'and he's ever so handsome; why he'll be my brother-in-law, soon, how wonderful!' All of a sudden though my thoughts changed, as his drifting eyes were taking on a new meaning, piercing my skin. I felt a cold naked chill tingle through my spine. Did he think I would be flattered? Was he just being nice to me? I felt uncomfortable and at the end of the dance excused myself and went to the powder room to brush away the thought that had put me on edge momentarily.

I went back to re-join the party that was starting to lazily leave the dance floor. People were gathering, as they do, to say their goodbyes. I hadn't quite reached the main throng of them, when Alistair walked towards me, and lifted my hand to kiss it saying:

'Pity we hadn't met earlier, perhaps I should do a swap with that brother of mine.'

Was there the tiniest moment of feeling flattered? Beautiful Maria, how dare he, or was I being too serious and this was just his sense of humour? Blushing in silence I moved to be at Jeremy's side. He was busy chatting with Tom and Sara.

'Fleur, darling, you've met Sara haven't you?' but his pleasant repartee was interrupted by a booming voice from across the dance floor.

'Don't know what you're doing with that brother of mine. Can't you do better than that?'

'Whoever is that?' mused Tom.

'You might well ask,' Jeremy replied, trying to mop up his embarrassment with a bit of humour. 'It's Alistair. Brotherly love eh?'

'I've heard so much about you, you know Fleur, and I think you've made a new man of Jerry, a bit besotted I'd say.'

'I can see why' Tom butted in, and so the conversation attempted to smooth over the Alistair comment as if it hadn't happened.

I went looking for Maria to give her a 'bye bye' kiss.

'Fleur love, it's been a good evening,' hasn't it. How are you? I've hardly seen you.'

'I know you look just wonderful Maria.'

'Mutual adoration society! Wish we'd had more time to talk. When are you going back?' I explained my ticket was for two o'clock the following day.

'Love you, give a hug to mother and father for me' Maria called.

'I will...' and my voice trailed off in the hubbub of the many bye byes.

I had booked in at a bed and breakfast very close to where Mandy was staying and so we shared a taxi. Jeremy told me he would see me later. It was such a relief to have that half hour journey of distraction with Mandy. I didn't know her but she was fun to be with and we chatted about the evening. Mandy's nana was from the North and she knew Settle well so that brought some kind of bond between us straight away and I thought it highly likely that we might meet again in the future.

Home for the night, I made myself a warm drink. I straightened the bed and hung up some of the strewn about clothes. I just had time to freshen up, squirt some perfume on and brush my hair down. The room started to smell of 'Coty l'aimant.'

The doorbell rang and in the late night air stood Jeremy. There seemed no time to speak: we moved into the stairwell. We had rarely had the chance to be so alone, and private; the rest is hazy. His mouth firm on mine was making love with a passion long awaited. This was the Jeremy I knew, and loved.

The silk of my dress hardly made a sound as it fell to the ground. Seeing the outline of my breasts through the finest French camisole Jeremy sighed 'Look at you you're beautiful,' Teasingly I helped him open the tiny pearl buttons of my top.

Released and free, taking my breast into his mouth, he suckled, and kissed it, then the other side. Unrestricted with all the time in the world the two of us faced the mirror, as he arranged my hair, to let it hang loosely over my shoulders. I turned away and rolled over onto the bed. The night was here. It was happening. This was serious.

I flinched as he slid his fingers purposefully up and under the hem of my long lacy petticoat and as he searched with a thousand kisses he covered my body. My shyness opened. My mind was alight; it was floating into the flickering candlelit room. I had never experienced a kiss like the one he was giving me.
 'It's so beautiful.' Laying back, his thumb nuzzled whilst his tongue, explored and deepened inside me.

'I don't want it to stop. It's so beautiful.' With hypnotic rhythm closer and closer we came together until I could stand it no longer. I caught my breath.

'No, no, I can't I cried, as I started to move away, but firmly, and determinedly Jeremy carried on just a little longer.

'No, no I can't.'

My pleasure too much, he stopped and with concentration written all over his sweating brow climbed back onto the bed.

Gripping onto the bars of the bed-head, I pulled myself up, to feel his weight and pressure pulsing in me over and over again. I felt I could burst and when the pace reached a momentum, I kept myself very still, the bed now shaking, we both cried out and his spluttering howl soared and spluttered again until the sweetest smell filled the room.

Stunned, and shivering, we pulled the duvet over us snuggling close. The silence now so stark, we heard the clock strike 1.0am and the hoot of an owl. Moments later, Jeremy returned to the room, bringing me a glass of water, to the side of the bed, he smiled and brushed my fringe away. 'You have such beautiful eyes, you know' I felt safe and so well loved. Overwhelmed and exhausted we lay curled round each other in the afterglow, as if too shy to speak, knowing what words couldn't say.

C8: Rings of gold.

The weekend of our engagement was very special and I remember thinking that mother and father really could see how much in love we were. Sometimes I thought mother had a faraway look, as if she was sad; was this simply the look that father used to describe as her beautiful gaze? Or was she sad in some ways that her daughters were grown up and now gone? There was just one gnawing thing that didn't feel quite right, but which I tried to reason off as being just one of those things. That was, no matter how close Jeremy and I were, the antagonism between Jeremy and Alistair was bound to make for strains and tensions between Maria and I that would have inevitable ripple effects through the family.

Jeremy was always kind and a friend to Maria, but this seemed to make for even more of an inflammatory situation between himself and Alistair. The brothers constantly rubbed each other up the wrong way. Alistair was forever coupling the fact that Jeremy was doing medicine with his being a snob. I could see difficulties for us looming and could not blow away the cobweb - that veil of growing doubt of two sisters falling in love with two brothers. I was determined that the differences in their ways of thinking and doing things would not drive a wedge through our hearts as sisters.

We were married on 28th June 1975 just nine months after Alistair and Maria.

We had a treasured few private family moments that I will always remember as belonging to our wedding day; mother, father, Maria and I had part of the morning together before Sara arrived (my other bridesmaid). Naturally we were busy, but we all had that together feeling of Springhill; we knew it and felt it, an odd cuddle, or rub of the arm.
`It's just lovely to see you both looking so well,' said mother, 'Fabulous! Grannie's old rocking chair: you've transformed it!'

'Wait until you see what's in here: the other rocker that we had at home from Grandma Lillian, remember? Choose between you which you want but they're for you both.'
Our father, with pride continued to show us his new toy, which was a rather smart camera, and he set it up so that he could be on the photograph as the camera flashed from the stand without him there to operate it. 'Cool!' We all laughed.

Before we knew it Sara was with us, straight from the hairdresser and always willing to help. Annie had telephoned to check that everything was going according to plan. The sun shone for us and mother looked very lovely in a powder blue dress and coat and a stunning mother of the bride hat. Then a significantly timed five minutes elapsed before the bridal taxi arrived and father and I stepped into it for that famous journey.

'Fleur, darling, you look so radiant. Thank you for being such a dear daughter,' he smiled shyly, turned to the window and got a handkerchief from his pocket.
'Feels a bit like going to school for that first time,' (I didn't know whether it was the big school or little one I was thinking of, neither really, words were just helping me out).

The beautiful dress, the ceremony, the joy and that moment of moments was about to happen:
'For better for worse,' when suddenly the step was there being taken. Father helped gather up the yards of lace train that belonged to my dress as I stepped out of the bridal taxi. I had never felt so much a princess. I loved my big sister Maria; she squeezed my hand so tight.
I loved processing into church, down the aisle to Jeremy. The church was packed and yet in some ways it was as if there were only a very few of us there. The things I particularly remember are the organ, the smell of roses, lily of the valley and polished pews. I remember the link of my father's arm with mine, the sight of who I was walking towards, looking at me as if he'd seen a vision from Heaven and then 'we are

gathered here'. The service and hymns, the photographs, the reception all went just fine and Jeremy surprised me by walking over to the microphone and singing to me!

'Take my hand, take my whole life too
Good old Elvis, how wonderful of Jeremy to croon away with a touch of his style to me,
For I can't help falling in love with you'.

The emotional coolness between the brothers continued, and I noticed there was a strain between their mother and father and them, but nothing was going to spoil our wedding day, and we were soon off on our honeymoon to Scotland.

We had less contact over the weeks, months and years. The tenderness to each other that Jerry and I knew, so evident to everyone, would, I thought, be like rubbing salt in to Maria's wound. Jeremy and I were rock solid. We adored each other and I felt I could trust him to the hilt; sadly though, I had already heard of Alistair's philandering. Jeremy was also aware and this increased his desire to keep a distance between them and us. What Maria and I hadn't realized was how we would be challenged by the complexities and strains around the relationship of our husbands; the loyalties we wanted to have for them amidst the love we had for each other. Maria and I were sisters who would love each other forever through thick and thin. I never let a bad word be said about my sister, I thought the world of her. It was mutual.

Alistair and Maria were living and working in London after they had married and were, like us trying for a family. I had known I wanted Jeremy's baby right from the very first time we made love. In that moment I had known, he was the one for me and I had secretly hoped, even imagined our having a couple of children. By this time, mother and father were retiring and decided to wind down into this next phase of their lives with a touring holiday before moving to Scotland. They were aware of sensitivities between their sons in law:

this caused them deep concern, but in their usual giving style thought that the best way to contend with the difficulties was to give everyone space. That 'going away' feeling was back and they decided to move on. They planned a route to see Europe before settling properly in Scotland.

The tests came back from the hospital and we both sighed. It was so hard, so difficult to think about, to know what to say, or do. It felt as if our life's plan had been snatched away from us. The doctor told us the fault lay medically no more with Jeremy than myself and it was just one of those things. Each of us tried to hide our disappointment and conversations would be interrupted when we worried where they might lead. Making love became full of sensitivities that hadn't been there before. We always felt so close, but the intense feeling of making love was so wrapped up in the idea of having a child, and had been replaced by the raw feelings of disappointment and failure.

It was Annie that came to the rescue of my mind, old Annie with her reassuring practical ways. Deep down my disappointment was there, but I could hear her saying we would be all right, there must be others in the same boat, and there were. I soon remembered Paula, Sophie, Ron and Moira. I wondered about them, would it be ok broaching the subject with them? For a while though, no matter how I put on my brave face, I wanted to cry, ring mum and pour my heart out to them both, but I couldn't: they were traveling, and it was their time to spread their wings too. In any case, it wasn't long before I was hearing some awful things about Maria, I was so worried for her.

I heard from Sharon, a close friend of Maria's that she was missing the conversations with mother too, the ones that were intimate and personal. Sharon said that when Maria did have an occasional call from her, it was stilted, as if hurt and concern hung in the air, mixed with mother's determination not to interfere. Maria and I spoke to each other less often too.

I had met Sharon at one of the parties and knew she would have Maria's interest at heart. She told me that Alistair had finished his affair with one of the secretaries at the office. She had got the impression when she last met up with Maria, that she had had some kind of inkling about the situation but had drawn a veil across it because of it coinciding with her pregnancy. Poor Maria, I felt helpless; it was all said in confidence so as not to make things worse for Maria, and this further tied my hands. I hoped at least to be a wonderful aunty to Maria's child.

It was later that we began to get a bigger insight into what Maria was suffering physically and emotionally. She tried standing her ground and looked to what she could do herself to improve, always prepared to take blame if there was any attached to her. She became increasingly at risk. She knew how contrite Alistair could be; sometimes he would ask for help (saying he could not understand why he was actively destroying the most precious thing that had ever happened to him) and then when the help came, it was a different moment and he would turn things into a mocking joke. Maria had taken her wedding vows seriously and was determined to try to find a way of being together, the more she took that approach, she unwittingly made him more powerful and herself, more of the victim.

C9: The moon fell from the sky.

The sun was shining, the morning that the letter arrived from mother and father, inviting us to meet up for a very small family celebration of their ruby wedding. The letter set out their quiet celebration plans, including the list of who was to be invited: Maria and Alistair, Jenny and Brian (friends from Scotland), and Sister Bernadette. They hoped to make it a 'happy and peaceful occasion.' Mother also wrote that there were things they needed to discuss with Maria and I on our own, so would need a couple of hours of our undivided attention for this.

There would be so much to tell them after all this time and so much to hear from them about their travels around Europe, partly by train and partly by air. For weeks I looked forward to this occasion, to seeing mother and father again. I ached to see them! I had missed them so much and yet in other ways felt happy for them and the plans they had of their own for the future, in this new phase of their life.

I knew they'd be missing us too, but believed stepping back to give us space and be independent was going to be good for us all. The reality was more difficult than any of us had imagined. We had so often thought how wonderful it would be when we were married with our different families coming together at different times with our parents, the reality felt full of unspoken tensions.

'Happy and peaceful.' Over the next few weeks that phrase in the letter played on my mind and I so hoped that it would definitely be a wish come true for us all on their wedding anniversary and that Maria and I would have the couple of hours on our own with them that they had asked for.

Nothing, but nothing could have prepared us for the shock that befell. It was one of the worst days of my life.

'Who on earth is this at six in the morning?' said Jeremy sighing as we both 'jumped', hearing the loud knock and persistent ring of the doorbell. We rushed downstairs.

'It's the police,' my high-pitched voice exclaimed as I pulled back the curtain by the front door.

Moments later a dreadful hush fell as we sat there stunned, drinking strong cups of tea one of the police officers had made for us. They had come to tell us the awful news. Our parents had been staying in a lovely glen-side hotel in Scotland with a small party of walkers. They had not returned for the evening meal and when they were not at breakfast the following morning, the guide contacted the police. I can still flinch when I hear that hollow sound at the door. Our parents were lost, missing, where were they?

As the story unfolded a sinister possible reality started to dawn, that they were more than missing. The last time they had been sited was on the way to sail their dinghy. Their growing passion about dinghy sailing had sparked off curiosity from others in the group. In fact we learned later at least two of the couples had been thinking of buying a dinghy for themselves.

Suddenly amidst the shock of this news, I remembered,

'O, my God! What about Maria?' I rang her immediately and she very sensitively heard the earth-shattering concern; the hardest news to give her. She was brilliant and in spite of her obvious distress was clearly relaying the news to Alistair whilst she was on the phone to me. They suggested, on the way they would call on Annie to give her the news briefly, in confidence and get her praying, whilst we would head straight for Glencoe and meet up with them there. At that point I really felt the love between the four of us, in action.

We hardly spoke, hardly breathed as Jeremy drove the longest journey of our lives to a scene I would never care to see again. By the time we arrived, ten hours from receiving the knock at the door, our parents would have been missing more than two days.

As we pulled into the hotel car park, silhouettes of two couples were awaiting us and purely from their postures in the late evening air we knew. Two bodies had been drawn from the loch. A strong current had forced the dinghy with gale force speed into and under a torrent of unforgiving water.

All our lives, Maria and I had sensed that awful sense of loss that mother and father knew through the death of our dear little Christopher, and now it was our turn to feel the knot and ill feeling of grief. Identifying mother and father, seeing them unrecognizable, is a memory of haunting capacity.

The moon fell from the sky.
Time stopped.
I don't remember.
We went to the police station.
I don't remember.

My legs were like jelly.
I couldn't speak.
When I did, it didn't sound like my voice.
We drank strong tea.

My eyes were open: I couldn't see.
Maria was here: God bless them.
They had come straight to Scotland.
We hugged; we cried.

I have no memory of the drive back and
'Goodbyes,' to the group.
Annie held the fort at home.
I don't know what she said.

I can see her white face.
I can see her red eyes.
I see the funeral director.
Mother and father are home again.

Someone has made a meal.
My tummy is bursting.
I am shaking my head.
Maria tells me to try to eat.

Maria has her arm around me.
I want to run away, to faint.
We are choosing hymns.
It is a pain beyond belief.

Maria, Alistair, Jerry and I were thrown together, in circumstances we could never have foreseen. Sister Bernadette showed her strength and believed that, 'the most dearly beloved couple had left this world together,' God had saved them facing their own parting from each other. In her eyes you could see her honesty, her torment, and resolve? But I couldn't take it in. Eerie echoes of mother's voice with her plans to see us, asking 'for a happy and peaceful occasion' resounded in my head along with the now cruel task we had to take on board, of planning their funeral. 'Unthinkable', I half wished it could be my own.

There were moments when I thought I saw them smiling. They would have been proud at the village, pushing the boat out for the much-loved Elizabeth and Dr. Andrews. A priest and vicar both presided. Movingly a group of patients gave a eulogy. Maria said a few words beautifully. I read a poem. We hugged each other. We chose our hymns. 'Make me a channel of your peace,' had to be one of them. In shock and hollow disbelief there we were, it was happening, we were walking behind two coffins to:

'Walk with me O my Lord, through the darkest night and brightest day, be at my side O, lord, hold my hand and guide me on my way.'

Going back to Springhill, which had been opened up for the funeral tea was just about more than we could bear and I could see Maria look lovingly and insecurely across at me with an expression that spoke volumes. Somehow we got through, and it was a great tribute to our wonderful parents. I found myself humming in my head:

Plaisir d'amour
Ne dure qu'un moment.
Chagrin d'amour
Dure toute la vie.

There are things in life for which there seem to be no answers; they are simply beyond our understanding, the ordering of events. We were so lucky to have had parents we loved so much, and felt so bereft without them. I felt we had lost pieces of our jigsaw. We realised how in the time when mother and father had gone away they had started to live their own life. I felt so pleased they had had that time separate from us, yet felt denied hearing about it all, what they had done, how they might have missed us too. I just wanted to hear their voices, tell them I loved them.

Whatever the strains from the Alistair and Jeremy situation, our parents' tragic death brought with the loss a new focus. Maria and I did have more contact. I took some comfort from deciding that Maria was being a loyal wife to Alistair and that being parents soon might bring Alistair to a new understanding.

Life ticked on and we found that our parents, in their meticulous and thoughtful ways, had left things well sorted for us, especially given that such an accident would never have been predicted. Mother's jewellery had to be shared. She had very little, but we loved what she had. The sapphire matching earrings and bracelet Maria was to have and I was to have the pendant. Mother, had always told us that a third of their money (the part that would have been Christopher's) would go to Sister Bernadette and her good causes.

'You have to stand on your own two feet and make your own way in the world, not have things on a silver platter.' Amongst mother's things there was Sister Bernadette's last letter to mother in which she said how glad she was about the pending celebrations and the arranged meeting with the girls and that she hoped to see mother before then if it were possible. 'What a shame that never happened,' I thought out loud.

There had been such a lot to sort out. Our parents had been travelling and had put much of their life from Springhill into storage. How strange it felt to-ing and fro-ing the impersonal storage container, instead of returning home to Springhill and the cooked dinners mother used to make. Annie was still there to give a helping hand. In the middle of the night in the quiet and darkness when thoughts take hold, I found it helpful to get up out of bed and pace the floor, look at an article in a magazine, or make a hot drink. Mother and father were gone, forever and ever.

'Come back to bed, darling,' Jeremy would say in a weary voice. How warming that was to hear, yet how difficult to feel settled ever again.

Polly wiped a tear away and put the book down. 'How awful,' she thought. Soon without realising it, Polly's own life was stepping forward in her mind. She thought of her loss and the void it created. She thought of the things she would have loved to say to Philip. She thought of the things she wished had never happened. She thought how much she loved Philip. She thought of her own skeletons in the cupboard? What a different opinion people would have of her if they knew.

She thought about the way she and Philip felt judged often for not having any children. Many might think they didn't want any. 'How wrong they'd be.' After years of trying for a baby and specialist treatment, it was Philip who showed the blues the most and Polly always thought he'd have been such a good, fun dad. Try as he could to hide his disappointment Philip used to assume it all to be his fault and for a while he became impotent. During all this, Polly knew they couldn't have been more understanding and loving but neither of them could really talk about how stuck it had made them feel. They sort of 'disappointedly' coped, filling the gaps doing things. This in turn would lead some people to have their opinions again with comments about them being 'driven' or 'restless', 'materialistic' even, because they spent more and more time on things to do with the house, or plans to move house. Why not? They were simply getting by, living their life, feathering their empty nest. Thank goodness, they also had some very good friends who knew them through and through.

When Polly looked up, she noticed a fresh face sitting opposite her having got on the train at the last stop. The woman looked up and smiled, some distraction welcome.
'This is going to Exeter?'
'I hope so,' said Polly. She picked up her reading, but within minutes had nodded off.
'Didn't you want Exeter?' The lady was nudging Polly who wakened to:

We are now arriving at Exeter St David's,
Please take all your belongings with you–

'What an amazing day we've had', Polly thought as she turned the key in the lock at home. Polly listened to her answer machine messages; Sam checking that she was OK because she hadn't returned any of her messages since early morning. She was so sorry about the re-arrangement. Polly smiled and thought if only Sam knew 'what I did instead'. Polly decided she wouldn't read that night; she was tired from her journey and could continue the following day. As she snuggled down, she thought about the dilemmas that faced Maria and Fleur and the tragedy that had befallen them. She thought of the whole notion of shame and how it affects the choices we make and the ways in which we recover.

She thought about the life she'd had. The same words would mean something different to Sandra. She thought of Philip, how she missed him. She thought how everything might have turned out very differently.

CHAPTER FOUR   BACK TO REALITY.

About 2am, Polly wakened and, after a quick freshen up de-
cided she'd make herself a warm drink and have another
read. 'One of the plus sides of being on your own' she
thought, 'you don't need to feel you are wakening anyone
else up!' They say 'a watched kettle never boils.' Whilst she
waited, she found herself brooding.

Bob at work, several years Polly's junior, was easy with the
compliments and thoroughly liked Polly in fact found her
attractive with her tucked in appearance, which showed off
the soft curves of her older body well. There was something
refreshingly honest about her, the way she dressed with con-
servatism yet confidence that although a bit mumsy had more
appeal for Bob than he had first realised.

Polly found Bob funny. He had the gift of the gab and at the
beginning she took anything he said with a pinch of salt and
yet under this bravado she thought he was charmingly
quirky, and she used to love hearing him talk about the three
little ones at home. She knew he had a very pretty wife and
would often hear him say what a lucky man he was. This
would be interspersed with the moments when he needed to
let off a bit of steam. There was a funny safe sort of security
about their friendship. Polly always thought reading between
the lines that he'd be rather difficult to live with. Thinking
back as she did brought quite a blur to Polly's eyes. She
could see so clearly now how such a collision of nothingness
in a way, had brought on these really strong feelings between
them. When was it that they started the longing for the mo-
ments they could snatch in the daytime to talk? When did
their feelings start to be sexually charged? She couldn't pin
point it and then one late afternoon, things started. There
was a moment of laughter, a lift in the car, Polly had found
herself very briefly touching Bob's knee in a comforting way,
he grabbed her hand, they looked at each other and the feel-
ing between them had become too hot.

Such a simple set of circumstances, ease of chatter, release of humour and time together had brought this disarranged pair together with all the charge imaginable. Polly didn't want to let herself think of the times she'd ache to see him, the pockets of moments they'd snatch to be in each other's arms, so their expression for each other could be let loose. There wasn't a single moment in this time of passion when Polly wanted to be with him forever, to break up his marriage or her own, and yet the stopping of something so spurious felt extremely difficult and was now so painful to reflect back on, not because it stopped, but because of how damaging it could have been if his wife or her Philip had found out. Feelings of guilt overpowered her at times. She really hated herself for it having ever happened.

The kettle was boiling.

The affair itself lasted eight months and although her guilt took some comfort in the fact that the sex had only fully happened four times, she knew that her unfaithful thoughts had gone on much longer. She also took some consolation in the fact that it was she who had brought the affair to a close. To her surprise Bob gave her no hassle, in fact, it seemed relatively inconsequential to him. Polly was relieved when two months later Bob's work took him to a different branch of the company, which meant they naturally had less contact.

Polly carried her story with her. She told no one about it. In some ways she and Bob had got away with it and certainly for her, it was a hot air thing that had blown her along for a while, but in other ways it haunted her, and she felt so angry with herself that it had happened. It was like a blot that couldn't be smoothed over and left her with uncomfortable feelings about lots of things. Philip was her man and always would be, and it pained her when he sent her the most beautiful birthday card and she felt choked up with the words. She was this person that he had chosen the card for, but did he really know her? Did she really know herself? Words once so right felt so wrong. How could she go on hiding to him what she had done?

Polly had always intended not going into retirement phase without telling Philip. She had a thing about honesty being all-important in a relationship and still believed that. She thought that when they were older it might be a better time to confess to him and that Philip might mellow through his hurt, into an understanding that more living and shortening of life might bring. She was both ashamed and frightened of telling him, because the consequences might be so big to face, and yet there was no alternative.

As life turned out the timing never seemed right and when Philip was diagnosed with cancer, devastating for both of them, it seemed that it was her ultimate punishment, so, until something triggered a thought she would lock these happenings away, almost denying they had ever happened. At work she would hear of someone leaving their husband or wife, for some affair or another, and would find herself looking shocked and joining the disapproving exclamations. What was she to do? Tell everyone of her own indiscretion? How easy it is to point the finger.

They had two really tender years. After the initial diagnosis, they got on with life in a way they hadn't done before, Philip much more actively arranging things to do together. They had one of their best holidays ever in Austria. They both loved walking and this holiday provided for time on their own and also joining up with a walking group for three of the five days there. Hard to think, that only ten months later his condition would have spread beyond repair. She climbed in her bed, mug of tea by her side ready for Maria and Fleur again.

Maria struggled on in her attempts to get things right. All she wanted was peace and things to work out. She was not a passive entity, she had character and vitality, but she had grown exhausted, brow beaten emotionally, and physically. Alistair frightened her; he was cold, contrary and cruel at times. I watched her increasingly eroded into a bland, blank screen on which he could imprint anything he liked. Maria was not self-righteous. At times when she danced to his tune, he felt all masterful and saw her beauty: he loved her and at other times the same thoughtful, considerate behaviour would trigger him to seeing her as a non-person who couldn't stand up to him. Alistair despised Maria in that moment seeing her as pathetic, like a walrus around his neck suffocating him; he wanted all the time to push her away, or goad her into a different response, her understanding ways driving him into further madness. But his contrariness was his weapon; she could never get it right for him.

There was a cupboard under the stairs into which she was pushed several times; no handle, no light, a trap from which only he had the power to set her free; standing up to him in that situation, screaming the inappropriateness of what he had done, pushed her further into the dark- a whimpering apology of some description from the cupboard was the only way back to daylight until the next time. No handle fitted on the inside of the cupboard would make a difference.

Sometimes standing up to him was the answer, other times; it brought blows usually around her head and face that on occasions landed her in casualty. He loved her face, but wanted to disfigure it. He wanted to protect Maria and see her suffer. There were times when Maria and I were on the phone to each other when I would sense I had rung at an awkward moment and Maria would hold onto the call and to me. She once told me she felt she had lost everything; she didn't pray, she couldn't sing, she had stopped making cakes. Even with all these difficult things, it seemed a wonderful moment hearing the news of baby Lily's safe arrival, perhaps this would make the difference that would really help them. No matter how much the mix of emotions was difficult to grapple with, I tried to set any of the negative thoughts aside. We drove straight away to the hospital. It was just wonderful seeing Lily for the first time, a fresh, beautifully blooming new born baby with a shock of dark hair and the tiniest fingers and toes I believe I had ever seen. Maria looked radiant, as if something exhausting but absolutely amazing had come to them, to be loved and cherished forever.

C10: Summer.

We would meet up three or four times a year.

So there we all were and having been at the graveside we decided to go for an afternoon tea before going our separate ways. 'Can hardly believe eighteen months has passed.'

We decided to travel together in Maria and Alistair's car. I sat in the back with Lily on my knee and Alistair got in the back with me. Maria was driving so Jeremy sat at her side in the front. I became aware of Alistair's gaze but held and concentrated on Lily.

'Looking good,' Alistair said his damp breath sending a shiver down my spine, whilst a swift hand rubbed my knee. A sickly feeling overwhelmed me.
'Poor Fleur, a child suits you,'
I hoped Jeremy would not hear his loud stage whisper, but the audience was meant to hear. I could stand it no longer.
'You!'
'You're even sexier when you get worked up. A pity you married the wrong stud.'
Everyone in the car was to hear that last comment. Maria turned around.
'GET OFF MY WIFE, YOU BASTARD' Jeremy shouted.

It was as if all those unspoken doubts and things we should have sorted out conclusively years ago had come bursting into the air.
Things were suddenly out of control.
There was a loud BANG.
The car hit the lamppost only missing another car by inches.
The car exploded.
It burst into flames.
 We were screaming and Lily cried,
 MMMUMMY

I heard the screeching of breaks.

The screams: the smash.
I heard the siren of police cars and ambulances.
My sister Maria is pronounced 'DEAD' at the scene.
My mind would not let me see her.
Pain was like a mountain.

'Why, why, why?'
There are no answers in the strange world that is collapsing
around me.
'Would you like a cup of tea?' a watery-eyed stranger asks.
How would I ever know what I'd like again?
Sick catches in my throat. I take a few sweetened gulps.

I climb into the ambulance to be with Jeremy.
He is beckoning me, 'Fleur, Fleur,' his face is pasty white.
'Darling I am here; you're going to be all right.'
He shakes his head, in the way immobile people can,
'I'm so sorry darling. I'm finished.'
We gaze at each other. It is like looking in a mirror.
'My lo', his unfinished words hang in the air.

I hear a single blood-curdling scream
'My Jeremy IS DEAD'
My control is gone.
Why could I not have died too?
It should have been Alistair.
Not Maria. Not Jeremy.
'IT'S NOT FAIR'.

It is happening,
I am not dreaming.

There was a blanket over a shape: it was Maria. There was
the sight of Lily jumping, wriggling, smiling, and crying.
Then I noticed the sight of a man standing close to Maria's
body with head bowed and an arm around him from comforters. Another piercing sound yelped free, and people were
looking at me as if I were going mad. The man by Maria was

telling them I would be all right; he would keep an eye on the child and me. The man sounding so concerned was Alistair. The comforters, ignorant of all the trouble he had caused, were comforting him. I opened my mouth and heard in my head a wolf howling, but the silence was stark. No glue or sticking tape could mend the answers without questions. There was no punctuation or order to anything.

A million years seemed to pass in time, our privacy invaded by giving statement after statement to the police. I asked an officer if there was a woman I could talk to alone, and within an hour this was arranged, for which I am eternally grateful. I didn't make a conscious decision not to give the details of the circumstances of the accident to the police, for where would I have started? It felt too complicated to go into too much detail as to what had happened. Lily couldn't have to add to her losses a dad in prison.

I was on automatic pilot: Lily needed me. Part of me was dead and had no voice. There was nothing to say: only things missing. Who was there left to understand?

Two separate funerals were arranged. There was also a memorial service for Jeremy held in the chapel at the hospital. I remember carrying a rose, and then things becoming fairly blank as if my mind could only cope with so much.

Plaisir d'amour ne dure qu'un moment

For I can't help falling in love with you.

Polly closed the book. She felt furious with Fleur for not having Alistair thrown into prison. She snuggled down as she mulled it over. It wouldn't be as easy as that, would it? she sighed! There would have had to be all the enquiries and what a stress and risk if it couldn't be proven. Feeling more understanding of Fleur, she went to sleep hearing the love and the pain in the plaisir d'amour tune. Polly found herself carrying the tune on as it changed to the words of Elvis's song 'For I can't help falling in love with you' She returned to the story.

Alistair was now sitting opposite me at our kitchen table. Lily was in her little chair sucking milk from her warmed bottle. Sometimes amidst hurt, another type of hurt happens that brings you to a new sense of reality: it happened to me. Feeling so stunned by everything I said little but had been thinking if he wanted me to bring up Lily for the first five years or so until he got settled I would do that. I just wished none of it had ever happened. Maria and I really had thought we were building bridges of a kind. What a mess! Maybe I should have told the police, but with Maria and Jeremy dead and feelings of loyalty and fear, how could I know what was best and right to do?

My focus was on what was best for Lily now. Would I have any say on behalf of Maria?

No, no, no, I screamed inside as I thought of it, I felt so desperately protective of Lily and again so helpless. One thing was a certainty that would never die and that was the love I had for Jeremy and my sister, I could cling on to that thought and that would help me cope. I would always be there for Lily.

Suddenly, all my heart searching came to a stop, because in one swoop Alistair reminded me of the mess he had brought to our family. Alistair leaned forward towards me. I looked back at him calmly, prepared to read as little into anything as I could. To my weariness I heard him say,

'Just you and me now babe.'

As if in the distance, with a silhouette of darling Jeremy standing in the room by my side, that feeling of nausea and repulsion returned that I had had in the car but imagining

Jeremy beside me, I grew strong, having stepped out of my body. In that moment, I was no longer alone.

'Why are you looking like that?' I am not sure what Alistair saw, or what he read on my face; I felt no fear, my grief ached, but the visualisation of Jeremy at my side was keeping me safe.

'You bastard, don't you think you've caused enough trouble?'

'Please, please Fleur you're just upset. Keep your voice down. Think of the child.'

Lily was crying. I thought I might burst.

'Think of the child? Were you thinking of her when you had the affair when Maria was pregnant?

Remember?

Were you thinking of her in the back of the car with me? Remember?

What about the child then?

Mr Gorgeous, is that who you think you are?

Is that what you think I'd think too?'

I picked Lily up out of her chair and made her a fresh bottle.

'You hadn't a clue about Maria and I had you? We were sisters who really loved each other. Was I ever flattered by your attentions? Not in a million years.

Know something?

I love your brother,

I love my sister.

I LOATHE YOU.'

At that moment, as if understanding the conversation, Lily started to cry.

'There you go again, see what you've done?'

I ignored this last comment of Alistair's, and opened the door.

'JUST GO PLEASE BEFORE I CALL THE POLICE.'

I was shaking.
Our grandmother always told us to keep our dignity.
His parting shot was aimed at me:
'OK, keep the little brat. Should have been a boy anyway, I'll send a cheque each month so you won't hold that against me too.'

I said nothing.

'Thank you Alistair; very kind!' He said mimicking my voice.

'Don't I even get any thanks? Sticks in your gullet does it that I can provide for my daughter?'

'Please, just go' I wailed.

'O, don't worry I am going. Can't you smell, or not bothered about hygiene eh? Thought a doctor's daughter might have noticed it needed its nappy changing.'

The SO and SO! Polly in her polite way was fired up, she wanted to leap into Fleur's life and sort Alastair out.

He was gone but for how long? His final parting comment became more helpful than hurtful to me; it helped me to see so clearly what Maria had had to deal with, it helped me, no end.

Polly swallowed, the trauma of the last few pages had been much harder to digest and had gripped and taken more out of her than she had thought. If this all really was someone's story, then who was Fleur and where was she? She noticed with interest for a while, that as she read, her own life had kept stepping forward, but now somehow she was back to thoughts of concern for Fleur and the family.

Polly could sense that feeling of responsibility that had lead Sandra to tell her all about it. What would they do? The book or manuscript was hardly something you would take to the police, wasn't it more something you would quietly take on board in a way Dr Gavin and Elizabeth would have gone about things? Maybe it should go in the shredder rather than land in the wrong hands and yet there was so much heart pouring and tenderness in the story, Polly was already wondering about Lily. It was certainly going to be no problem to complete the reading before Wednesday. The bigger issue would be thinking what to do with it for everyone's sake.

C11:   Tender Love.

I kept a photograph up of Maria and would take Lily in my arms and we would point 'mummy' to it. Lily thought her daddy had gone away to get work. When Lily cried, sometimes they were such deep tears for her mother, the pain ripped through my heart and we hugged and in a way grieved together. Her childish way and lack of inhibition helped me every bit as much as I helped her. Gradually as time went on, she asked less for 'mummy,' but we always kept certain rituals in memory of her, and I was always aware that she might have to leave me one day. I knew her father might come back for her at any time. Our relationship was dreadful but I had no real reason to believe that he wouldn't be able to provide for Lily or even be a dad to her in his own way.

I kept a photograph of Jeremy, and myself at my bedside and took so much comfort from it. For months and months I would pick the photo up on awakening and going to sleep, greeting it in a way that could help start or complete the day. We looked so happy; it was taken on the green, by the bridge at Burnsall at their country sports day. Night after night the bed felt so empty, I could beat my pillow, or cocoon myself, wrapping the eiderdown and bedspread around me, but nothing would ever bring him back. I sat up straight, I must remember: there was a new little heart to love and love her I did, unconditionally.

Lily had a loving nature and people who had known Maria would comment sometimes how like her mother she was. For the first year of our being alone, without Jeremy, Maria and my parents, we had the love and support of several close friends; Catherine, from the library and her husband were extremely supportive and loving to us both. Tim was marvellous at playing with the two or three finger glove puppets that I had made for Lily. He would pop them from his pocket or above the back of the settee, his voice sounding as light as a fairy one minute, as gruff as a giant, or as bleating as a lamb the next minute. Lily particularly liked the cuddly lamb puppet, and would do her best to bend her voice to a bleating sound, which sent her into giggles.

Annie was a marvel, coming to see us Monday, Wednesday, Friday, and at the weekend she would come along for the afternoon on Sundays. The regularity of this in that first year meant a lot. She was truly my 'treasured' link to Springhill.

We had decided to live near Pen-y-dale after we were married because Jeremy had a job at the cottage hospital and thought it was important to live a little bit away from work and so we settled into our home on the edge of Waddington. Little did we know at the time, the tragedy that would befall us. I was ever glad though to be in that area, which was semi-rural, yet in easy access of local village facilities: a small local school, church, library, and in the village, there was a thriving corner shop. There was a walkway through the centre with the memorial gardens. I so loved the community spirit, which never felt too intrusive but was always supportive. At the library I was able to fill in with relief work, which lead up to regular part-time and eventually full time employment.

Annie was a great friend. I used to collect her from her home and bring her wheelchair with us, and she would keep an eye on Lily for me and tell her a story, like no one else could. She was wonderful at knitting, so Lily was always well supplied with cardigans and for Christmas Annie had made her a hand knitted rag doll: she loved it. Lily called her rag doll Su, and Su and Lily went everywhere together for a while. Sometimes, Annie and I would do 'reminiscing' together, but we wouldn't dwell too long on things - we couldn't, though we somehow got to know a little bit more about each other.

One day I started to cry, I am not sure what had triggered it, but Annie was there to comfort me, and I told her how sad I was that Lily was growing up without a father and mother.

Annie reminded me what a good mother Lily had in me and then slowly, Annie, rocking in the chair started to unintentionally unravel the stories from her own childhood, just in snippets.

'There, there, my love, Lily will be all right, there is much love around her, so there is, and yes it is so sad for a child not to have a parent whether they've died, or are not there in one shape or another; the main thing is to have some understanding of the situation and to make sure the child is shown love. In my case, I grew up with a dad who was more missing than he was present.'

'Annie darling, here you are,' and I passed her the tissues.

'Poor mother, she was in one of those traps, I can still shiver when I think about it.

Maybe he couldn't help it, but it was awful.

Right from being around Lily's age, I learned to keep a distance from him. We'd freeze when he came in, his presence made everything seem so different. Even the animals noticed the tension, yet still now with these older eyes, I often find myself trying to understand.

Maybe going to war, being amidst such barbaric times, and seeing friends blown apart had made him shut it all out in his mind, the thoughts being too much to cope with.

Maybe the holding back of all the emotion in his heart, made him feel all the more that the day-to-day living with a family at home was trivial.

Maybe, maybe.'

Maybe, being Annie, his daughter, meant it was natural for her to keep searching for explanations.

Several cups of tea later, with tissues on the fire, Annie was telling me how Danny had returned home finally from the First World War when she was eleven years old. It was as if he could not handle anything emotional, so stuck to being sarcastic, wrapped up in 'I'm only joking.'

'Could never feel right bringing friends home'.

'Annie, darling I had no idea.'

'I know, here I am at eighty and it's still on my mind, it's weird but I do sometimes feel sorry for dad, I was his daughter and I never gave him a hug or anything like that. Anyway enough of me, you have enough on your shoulders without having to comfort old Annie here. I just wanted you to see that people grow up and make good of what they can. We had a good childhood, as good as our circumstances allowed. I'll never know if not going to war would have made any difference or not. It's one thing feeling sorry for me, for him too, but my mam...' at that she sobbed as she rocked thinking of her mam.

'So, so lucky to have met Harry, that I was, so glad for our Susan and Billy. Don't you go worrying yourself about the bairn; she'll be fine, you'll see.'

So that was how Lily and I grew together, accepting our situation. I started to live for every moment I had with her, and I tried not to look too far ahead, and I never ever forgot old Annie's motto of keeping independent thinking, because in some ways aren't we all alone in life?

Annie and I both knew not to rely on one another too much, and knew that inevitably there would be another parting, but this predicted pain could not stop our need to be in touch the way we were. When it happened we would cope and we did.

It was the fourteenth of November 1981 when Annie died peacefully in her own home. I had been standing at her door knocking for well over the hour and was concerned at the tell-tale sign of the milk bottle still on the doorstep. I had left my keys at home, not expecting to find the door locked. Two hours later that seemed like an eternity, the police broke into the house only to find the worst: Annie on the floor, dead following a heart attack. We'll never know what had happened just before her fall, but in that deadly silence, Susan and I rocked and comforted each other and both of us found ourselves chatting out loud our thanks to her for all the things that had been so hard to put into words for such a long time. Susan and I had been expecting it to happen for a while, but in the here and now of the moment, it was still a shock we didn't ever want to happen. Annie had been noticeably frailer over the winter months and appreciated the hot pot I would take her. She had reached eighty-one when she died.

Harry, gone all those years ahead of her, had left instructions of what he hoped would happen, when Annie's time came, to celebrate the life of such a remarkable woman, wife and mother. He had left in his rough handwriting an inscription for it to be said of her 'she was my life's treasure. We were all moved that he had put his heart into words for her long before he died himself. 'Treasure,' indeed that was so very true of both Annie and Harry, and it was true that you couldn't think of one without thinking of the other.

I still miss her and can't think of her without smiling.
Polly felt full to bursting.

Somehow we carried on. We would remember in the memorial gardens, which ran through the centre of the village. We would remember when Lily tried humming something and we would look at each other, as it was an Annie tune. Lily was soon bringing her friends home for tea and she would often remind me of my sister Maria. Lily was probably going to be taller than Maria, but she had the same lustrous hair and her mother's heavy lidded beautiful eyes. As I looked at her, sometimes I would catch a look of her father too, and even of myself, and Jeremy.

As time went on I wanted to reach out to what I could of the past for the sake of Lily, and I suppose also for both of us. I remembered that Lily's paternal grandparents had come to the funeral. I had only met them three times in my life before that awful day, once, at our engagement; the second time was at Maria and Alistair's wedding and then our own wedding. I had been so resistant to contacting them on my own, because my mind had been dwelling on Alistair, but then I remembered they were also the parents of my Jeremy and what is more important they were the only living grandparents Lily had. It didn't take long to arrange a meeting that soon became a monthly occurrence and one, which we got to look forward to.

On our first visit Granny Madeline and Grand pops were rather formal, though clearly delighted to meet us. I had not prepared myself for suddenly seeing photographs of Jeremy and Alistair placed on the same dresser, but of course, why not? They were both their sons after all, and then there was a photo in a small frame of Jeremy and me, I gulped. George was especially attentive to me, showing a lot of empathy to the stress of my personal situation, with the sudden losses of my parents, my sister and my husband. He reminded me of Jeremy, although when his mother smiled, her cheek dimpled, and that was a Jeremy thing too. There was guardedness as to what they said about Alistair, perhaps they thought Lily would be listening 'all ears', whatever. I could just sense that their concerns about his unpredictable behaviour went back a long way. Madeline turned to the photograph of Jeremy and me.

'He was such a good son'

'Come, come, dear, we must think about the child,' George said softly to Madeline.

'It's all right; you must both miss him so, so much.'
'O, Fleur, we do, we most certainly do.
What about you?'
'I want to wee,'
Never was such a moment more welcomed, as Lily jiggled, needing to be shown where the toilet was and we all were relieved to smile.

'Come on little Miss Moffatt, let's show your m...' something stopped him from completing the 'Mummy' word.
'I think Grand pops wants to show little Miss Moffatt where her tuffet is!'
'Toilet,' said Lily.
'That's right. All right Aunty Fleur will show you.'

Gradually we got to know each other better and I heard more about the strains between the brothers; it had been a long-term problem.
'Very difficult to manage as parents, they were just different you see,' was all Madeline would say.
'Never really got on the boys you know,' explained George. They wondered where they had gone wrong.

They were happy for me to sit quietly and listen as they heard their own words, and possibly spoke more openly through their grieving and loss than they had done before to each other about these difficult thoughts and feelings that they shared about their two boys. They told of times when Alistair had shown a sweeter side of his nature, but always spoke as if the rest of the time he was not quite normal. Could they not have thought Alistair was just a little less expressive than his brother, or perhaps a little clumsier? Would that have made any difference? Increasingly it was sounding more that the boys had grown up, one being seen as 'good,' the other 'bad'- such an easy knot to get into and so difficult to disentangle from once it has happened in your head as parents.

'One and a half sugars is it, dearie?' Granny Madeline asked, possibly noticing my distant look as she handed me another cup of coffee. I started to be more relaxed on our visits to grandma and grandpa, and used to enjoy the times when one of the grandparents would take Lily out walking, as she pushed her dolly in the pram. This gave me a little time for a rest and one to one chat with the remaining grandparent. 'I am so glad that Jeremy chose you dear for his wife, you're so well matched you know. He was over the moon to meet you, my dear,-the love of his life.'

The knock at the door came when Lily was six. She was a chirpy, quietly spoken little girl, with hair that fell in ringlet curls. The knock came louder and sharper. Why was my heart shaking?
Lily started to run towards the door. I stopped her just in time with; 'Sit down Lily.'

To my horror, the nightmare I had always dreaded was happening before my very eyes; Alistair was standing there, in our sitting room, with a grin on his face, and there was a young woman by his side. 'Just thought I'd call to let you know I have married again.' The woman smiled at him.

'Well, where is she?' He asked, as he walked further into the room. To my horror, he scooped Lily up in his arms.
'Hello there princess, remember your dad?'
'Daddy! It's my daddy!' said little Lily excitedly opening the present he had passed her. She popped the pink monkey puppet snugly on her hand and waved it about teasingly to each of us in turn.
'I love Mr Monkey.'
'There'll be plenty more where they came from,' said Alistair who seemed genuinely pleased to be seeing Lily again and showing her off to his wife.

'We've come to take you home with us, you can come and see where Mr Monkey's other friends live.' Lily looked shy and a little uncertain.

'You might have rung to tell us you were coming.'
'So you could have cleaned the house and plumped up the cushions?'
'So I could have prepared Lily.'
'Prepared her, what for? To give you time to poison her mind, is that what you wanted? Give me a chance Fleur, she

is my daughter after all and I did say I'd be back someday. Marianne is a good mother; she's expecting in June, so that'll be nice for Lily.'

Like a robot, my hands quietly continued gathering some of Lily's things.

'Come on Lily, darling, Aunty Fleur is just going to get that little bag of things ready for you.' This day had been hanging over our heads for ages.

'You had your chance.'

I held as much of a smile as I could muster, in response to the waving Lily was doing to me with her outstretched puppet hand, which rose over Alistair's shoulder; her eyes looked full to the brim and for me...time stood still.

The door closed and Lily was gone.

I was never to see or hear of her again, at least not until much later.

Mr and Mrs Parks were speechless about it all and so, so sorry for me. I missed them too, but all I could do was encourage them to be in touch with Lily. Eventually I learned they had moved to the south of France.

*

C 12 I picked more daisies.

Alone again: without our Lily to love I was entering another lonely phase of my life. One night, I thought of Maria so much and I felt so angry that I had let the poor relationship between the brothers and Alistair's inappropriate advances towards me make for such potential strains between Maria and me. Yet, I remembered that through all the difficulties and however far apart we had been, we had always managed to know we were there for each other.

I really loved my sister.
I missed her.
I ached for Lily.
I missed Jeremy so much.
I missed my mother.
I missed my father.
If someone had said: 'you can die tomorrow,'
I would have said 'Please.'
I felt I had had enough and wanted to simply fade away.
For who was there left to really miss me? This thought would keep circling my mind. Somehow life carried on.

'They were just sailing, quietly enjoying the day and then they were gone. We were just sitting in a car and then it was all over.' I would torment myself with these repeated thoughts. During this time I was at risk of becoming more and more reclusive, as I started to fear almost any form of travel. For a while my main method of getting about was walking.

In this incredible abyss, I discovered I would learn or re-learn to love trees and hills and flowers and notice more the sunlight on water, all the things we so much valued together as a family at home. The hill would be there tomorrow when I woke, the frosts would come and after a blanket of snow, the daintiest of flowers, snowdrops and primroses would pop through the earth in clusters, people would say 'like miracles'. These things are miracles, and now I could choose to notice them more. All of these things brought back to me, in small waves of warmth, my fond relationships as I remembered them. I would now be more likely seeking things to love about situations, as well as and rather than fixating on people, exclusively. Close relationships felt like a 'no, no' as I felt that I could not face the pain and stress of losing again. So I went for walks.

I celebrated the things of nature around me.
I celebrated knowing God through nature.
I celebrated having been brought up by two adoring parents.
I celebrated having the best sister in the world.
I celebrated the joy of polishing a table: seeing it shine.
I celebrated having been married to my dear husband.
I celebrated hedgehogs: Nana Hastings' knee.
I celebrated the time sitting next to Grandma at the piano.
I celebrated Annie and Harry.
I celebrated Sister Bernadette.
I celebrated my time with Lily.
I celebrated the stars.
I celebrated the moon.
I picked more daisies.

The little stray black cat that arrived on my doorstep, I called Boss. I loved him dearly. He needed feeding each day, needed me to get up in the morning for me to let him out. So time passed and I grew old gracefully.

There were several gentle, sometimes sweet advances made towards me over the years. These were mostly flattering, and gradually I could feel warmth again and smile. However, the memories of Jeremy, mother, father and Maria were so strong in my mind that I found a new way to be in my emotions towards other people, so that I felt comfortable with them. I met several people who had lost their husband or wife, and learned how much we all pick ourselves up in different ways. I started to feel I was in the world again and that I could be happy again. I remained safe. For now, this was a higher motive; perhaps it is another way to be loved. I was able to look backward and forward to see and find love in all sorts of ways. I found myself giving out cooler messages than I sometimes felt inside, sometimes with an apology because I never wanted to hurt. I did provide a shoulder to cry on, and was surprised just how often my shoulder was used!

I suppose I had kept my looks. I could have written a book about some of the tales men would tell me, maybe to get some sympathy from a lady on her own who had a lovely face and a well preserved figure and most of all had the sort of ears that could hear without always talking, moaning or interrupting, and who could be sure always to hold their conversation in confidence. My celibacy kept me safe, for a while anyway.

On the whole I found men's company easier than women's, but there was nothing new in that. I started to learn a bit more like a child again. I found a way of brightening some moods. When I was beginning to get stuck in my thinking, I would switch to similar, but lighter words for example; 'I am feeling so depressed,' would become 'think I'm perhaps just having a 'topsy/turvy' day today.' Or 'just feeling a touch melancholy', and this would lead to much more lovingly disposed behaviour towards myself, and through to lighter thoughts, rather than the darker words of depression. I found with this 'second chance' approach, I could trust much more that somehow I would get by and give myself the chance that tomorrow might come and I might feel better. I wondered, how someday it might happen that I made the transition from being so guarded relationship wise to having relationships again.

Maybe it was that plane journey.
After the capsizing of the dinghy, Maria and I had both always meant to go for a sail together because we both knew deep down that's what sometimes you need to do, to face your fears. By the time I got round to it Maria was dead.

I made a plan. I was alone in the world. The only way I could carry out the plan was to do it alone, to tell noone. In some ways it was as if I didn't even tell myself.

I remember selecting the date, and decided that the risk of travel would be neither in a dinghy, or a car but I would experiment with a plane journey. I remember booking the ticket and paying for it. I had no idea how I would feel but just knew it was necessary to do it. I recall the day I completed my secret mission by getting a taxi to the airport and the long time it seemed waiting for my flight to be called. It was about six months before I met Paul.

Travelling with just a small bag holding the lightest overnight things, but carrying the heaviest stone in my heart I boarded. I felt so cold, so alone, too curled up to speak. I looked around the plane, wondering how near take-off I could change my mind and disembark. Everyone else seemed to be jollying ready for some holiday. I was stuck; no way out from now. It was something I had to do, no one was telling me, and yet the feeling was that there was no choice, though deep down I always knew it was my choice.

In the middle of 'if only' thoughts;

'If only our parents hadn't gone for the sail that day,' I became aware of a passenger moving into the seat at my side. I only heard the repetition.
'Sorry, did you hear me? Are you happy with that seat or would you rather sit in the aisle?'
I didn't look at him but just muttered that I was OK.

The mystery man soon got the measure that I wasn't wanting to talk and maybe that and the anxieties of the situation in a way brought on some surprising sexual tension between us, and got me thinking all of a sudden of the film Brief Encounter. I could smell the warmth of his woody aftershave, and in a way this helped to airlift me to a totally different place in my mind. Gradually with a prolonged flight where we had had to disembark the plane and get back on again, we broke the ice and chatted about all sorts of things. I did not let a moral mind question my momentary pleasure; I was being propelled. It was such an achievement to be making that journey that if anything, my mixed up thoughts and emotions were disconnected, suspended. I had transformed the man at my side into the Angel Gabriel himself and a film starry one at that, perhaps even sent from Heaven by Jeremy. I found myself for the first time in my life, not caring about any of his personal circumstances: whether he was married or not, and so I found myself deliriously receiving his phone number at the end of the trip and more than that, agreeing to meeting up with him, the following week.

Wednesday night came and there I was, anxiety about a flight was a million light years behind me, and instead I was putting on my makeup, noticing myself in a way I hadn't done before. I knew nothing of this man and yet I felt unconstrained with him and as I brushed my hair, I looked sideways at my figure, breathing in as much as possible. I waited for my mystery man for an hour and twenty minutes offering to myself every excuse under the sun for his not coming until the penny dropped that maybe just maybe I had been stood up. I rationalised that if he was married then he had decided to do the right thing and not complicate his life or mine by turning up. Perhaps his wife was in a wheelchair and for a moment he had wavered, maybe he was recovering from some painful divorce, maybe he had panicked. Extraordinary isn't it, how we explain things to ourselves.

It was around this time that I started to take an interest in adapting clothes. I had always been somewhat artistic but this new playfulness that came my way allowed me more freedom and confidence to experiment with clothes too. I wasn't launching myself as a designer or anything like that. Annie had always had a needle and cotton, pair of knitting needles to hand and I started to realise how absorbing it could be, in a really positive way, to have on-going projects; something to start and finish, to fill in idle moments, and take your mind off things.

Angela's mum had taught me how to relax with material too, how to enjoy putting it this way or that, cutting a bit off, stitching a bit on and standing back 'to see what you were creating.' We always had fun at Angela's that was the thing, and nothing could ever really be a disaster; it would just be turned into something else or end up in the bin. Several times when I admired a summer frock Angela was wearing; she would laugh and say something like, 'Aunty Jenny's living room curtains!' So it felt great now to be reconnecting with this practical hobby. My sewing would be there the next day, would neither die nor walk out on me and though I might obsess about it a bit, there were so many spinoffs. I started to see colours in new ways. I had always loved the countryside so rich in its different colours and seasons. I always loved Monet for that reason. Yes a mixture of all of these things gradually helped to refocus my mind and to shed the claustrophobic feelings that had accompanied my tight chest, and

I began to breathe in this new kind of fresh air.

Bring Down the Moon

CHAPTER FIVE   THE WHOLE WORLD HAD GROWN.

I started to welcome living on a shoestring and shopping around charity shops. In fact I took a job just one half day a week working in one, and loved the times I could arrange the window and put things together in a different way, tops near skirts where the colour would not necessarily conventionally 'go' yet somehow it worked. It was great to see how ideas would start to catch on, and customers would seem to go home satisfied with their purchases.

One year during this particular cameo of time I looked at travel brochures for trips to Tuscany, and although I didn't go there, from my reading about it, I absorbed the imagined thoughts of being there. I could whisk myself there in a moment and soak up the atmosphere, the culture, the richness of the language, the terracotta earthy colours so vibrant and Mediterranean. I used to dream of sleeping under the stars. The new lease of life I entered expanded my view on things so much that I never lost it once I had found it. It reminded me of the song, 'Some enchanted evening' and yet I could hum that song thinking how 'the stranger' didn't have to be a person, it could be an idea, a love of something that would fly to your side.
'Some enchanted evening, you may see a stranger, you may see a stranger across a crowded room. Then fly to her side and make her your own or all through your life you will dream of your youth.'

Something really did seem to happen to me in my thinking during this growing or awakening or rebirth into the world around me in a new way. I wasn't so hard on myself any more, I could make a conscious effort to remember giving myself those second chances, not getting stuck as much or preoccupied with one particular thing. It fitted well also with my love of music. Like music, my thinking could be a little more liquid, adaptable alongside my spirit and my spirit could adapt alongside it too. I noticed how some days the colours I saw seemed to be darker, less vibrant than on other days; the walk by the stream didn't seem to have the sparkle from the sun dancing on it, or maybe I didn't notice it, but then there might still be a way I could take something back from that walk with me. I might even think later that night; 'I didn't see the sun sparkle on my favourite stream today'. And then this message to myself would help me realise I was a bit down and it would be time for a warming hot chocolate or a phone call to one of my friends. How amazing!

I was very reflective in this stage of my life and had become acutely aware of how much one can accumulate in a lifetime. I could have a therapeutic de-clutter.

I remember one day going into work wearing a home sewn skirt, complete with raw edge worn in a layer over another skirt, which showed a little beneath the other. It felt comfy and breezy and I enjoyed wearing it - it didn't particularly bother me what other people thought or if it went by with no comment. Several people simply said: 'You look good today.' Barbara Bailey whispered to me:
'Did you know your hem's down? You can slip home at lunch and change if you want to.' Two years later raw edges hit the high streets and I remembered Barbara and wondered if she remembered me too!

Polly was giggling. A lot of this could have been her shop.

The years rolled on and I imagined that Lily would now be grown up, with children of her own, perhaps. What a sad life to lose her mother as a baby, and later to have lost her aunty; never to know her grandparents well. What a lot of loss she'd had. I had to stop my galloping thoughts. I thought how much Maria would have loved being a grandmother. I thought of my dear Jeremy.

I thought with a new curious affection about the whole business of Maria marrying Jeremy's brother and how the two brothers, two sisters situation had brought with it far more complexities than if we'd belonged to separate families, and yet I could also see how non interfering both sets of families were almost to a fault and how if the boys had got on well, how it could have been brilliant to have the closeness. I thought how each family feeds on stories and hand me downs from the past putting their own spins on things. I recalled dear Annie telling me in the kitchen at home, how somehow we just get by and grow up anyway.

I thought of how encouraging and helpful my friend Sara's mum was, and how when she put things aside, for example to help her with a Christmas box of food, how loving and kind this was seen to be. However, when our mum started to do the same for Maria first, and later on for me, it ran the risk of being interpreted as her being controlling, patronising in some way - her good intention snarled up, disqualified through some critical eyeglass of privilege, her gesture being interpreted as lording it over us. I started to understand the role and importance we give to 'the perceived other' in our lives.

From my new position I could look forward and backward with greater calm and less defensiveness. I was able to really love my childhood again and its many associations, and see it as a potpourri that had made some things seem easier to learn than others. In the main, having gone through the many hoops of reflection over the years, I was settling at seeing it as special again but in a more ordinary way, for setting aside the frills that other people saw, the real riches of our upbringing went much deeper; in the stimulation, time, music and love that was given to us by parents so freely. It was obvious to us that they loved each other. I had gone through a phase of thinking all sorts. I had thought for a while how silly, or inadequate Maria and I were and now was able to remember once more what accomplished young women we once were.

From time to time I found myself seeking out church. Maybe there was some sort of security in some of the rituals. Maybe it was the annual visits to Sister Bernadette, or the quiet influence of my mother's stories about her home life, I don't really know and don't need to analyse; but seeking structure, prayer, and solace seemed to help. The candles and the singing were warming to me. I would usually leave a candle or two continuing to burn for special intentions at the end of the service. I got used to lighting the candle and letting a higher spirit around decide what I had lit them for; I told myself this prevented me from getting too maudlin.

One of my friends was a young priest, Father Tim. He was so tall and handsome with the clearest of blue eyes and most radiant smile, it made one wonder however he had made it to being a priest. His caring relationship became stabilizing to me, and was important to both of us. We would discuss the news of the day personally, and what we read in newspapers or on the television. We would share what books we were reading.

I remember telling him in detail about: 'Girl with a Pearl Earring,' a book that held me in its grip. I loved it as a story of sensitivity. I loved it for the gaps in between the lines that gave me room to daydream in my own thoughts, in a different way to anyone else's so that it became a story for me. We would talk about music and listen to it sometimes together, and in that listening something would happen in our connection beyond words. To be together simply and quietly listening to music is a wonderful almost divine sort of thing.

C13   Portrait of Lily

10.01.2005

On the 10th of September 2005 there was a knock at the door and there stood a young woman, an almost Pre-Raphaelite vision, very pale and willowy with lush long hair and a dress with a smocked top that hung loose on her long limbs.
'Aunty Fleur?' It was Lily.

I could hardly catch my breath, but managed to contain myself. We hugged with an initial reserve. What would it be like after all this time? What had she come to tell me? Sometimes I so wished I could for a few moments be someone without a care in the world, not always weighed with careful thoughts of consideration for other people's needs. With that minute of hesitation over we were in each other's arms. I could see both her mother and father in her.

As if to prove her identity, Lily was wearing the sapphire earrings that her mother had loved. What a beautiful young woman Lily had become; she looked of delicate, serious persona, and yet there was an ethereal lightness about her, and she had a softness in her eyes, which was compelling, and as she spoke I heard echoes of the little girl I had known. Her distinctive slight lisp was still there, not obliterated with the sophistication of adulthood and passage of time, but a visible cobweb, an audible link which had a charm of its own. All these years had passed between us, but with the speed with which we were catching up, you would think it was only yesterday that we were in touch.

It wasn't long before Lily's father came into the conversation; she told me that he had gone to live in Molyvos, on the island of Lesvos. This news helped me to calm down, and freed me to talk about things that needed to be spoken of, and more hugs followed. According to Lily, the beautiful fishing port seemed to have brought a restorative influence to Alistair, making him more reflective of his life, his mistakes and more poised for a simple future.

'He and Marianne never worked out; but it didn't really bother me, because being at Lady Moore's from eleven meant I had only holidays to sort out and granny and grand pops were brilliant, they were my main 'home' supports, even after they moved to France.'

'I am so glad you stayed with them.'

'Yes, you know what dad's like, on another planet most of the time. He makes me feel about one inch tall or non-existent. But then I suppose...' she shrugged,

'I try to remember about mum and everything, you know, maybe he misses her? It must have been a shock, the crash and that's how I try to sort of understand him and sort of forgive him for being a bit weird because of mum.'

Part of me, as her aunty, (her mother's sister) wanted to speak up; part of me had my mouth open without the scream coming as I heard Lily saying, 'he's just on another planet.'

Part of me left the unexplained unheard, and remained listening, for part of her was part of him and I was not in her shoes.

'He's got a new woman on the go, she's called Olga and so far so good, they've been together for the past three years. She doesn't speak much English, but they seem to get by, and her family is close at hand: they see dad as a provider for Olga and quite a catch.'

'I see, now Lily, not meaning to butt in, but would you like to come out with me now, or would you prefer to have a rest? I need to take Bumbles for a walk. She gets a bit fractious if I leave her too long.'

'Ah, Bumbles, she's gorgeous! How old is she?'

'Well, I've had her three years and she was four when I got her, so yes she'll be about seven. Come on Bumbles!'

'I love her coat; she must take so much grooming.'

'Well, it doesn't seem like that, but I suppose that's because I just keep on top of it and I got three scarves last year from her for Christmas presents.'

'Scarves?'

'Very soothing it is. I first learned to spin following a holiday away up in Scotland, and ever since then decided at some stage to find a loom. The way it happened, the loom found me, or it came along with this cottage.

Sorry, Lily, you were saying about your dad?'

'No really, Fleur, this is fascinating; I'll get back to that later. So go on, I never thought you were an animal person.'

'Well, I suppose I am really. We always had a family dog and Annie (who we grew up with) she had chickens and a donkey, and goat, so I suppose the affection for animals was in my blood. Anyway, the main thing with Bumbles is, she belonged to my dear friends Angela and Simon, but when they moved to Australia, they decided to find a good home for her. They knew I had a soft spot for Old English Sheepdogs, so that's that. She has such a sense of humour and well, she's just Bumbles.'

'So, did you know her when she was a puppy?'

'Yes, I met her twice, and she really was a darling, but I prefer her now. She's just like a gentle giant sized teddy bear. Down you go! Think you're being talked about, do you?'

'She's very intelligent, and a'

'…proper scally-wag! You're right there; especially if she decides she wants to play with the hens! We'll just join up to that top lane and then do the loop back to the cottage. That'll do you for today Bumbles won't it?'

It was so lovely walking with Lily and Bumbles. I told her about the six hens and it meant so much telling Lily about these hobbies and interests that had become part of home in Devon to me over the years. The hens and Bumbles really did take up quite a bit of my spare time and were tying but worth every moment as far as I was concerned. We were soon back, at the gate to the cottage, and whilst dressed and wrapped up in our outside gear, I took Lily to see the hens.

'Don't tell me you've got names for them all!'

'No, I haven't but I can tell them apart, and they do enjoy being picked up and cuddled. See that little one over there has been a bit down recently.'

'Fleur!' Lily mused at the thought of a hen being a bit depressed.

'No, seriously, look how her head goes to one side. There, I got them from the rescue place, and have learned as I have gone along, and with what I remembered from Annie. I already had this hut, so just got the perch and nesting boxes fixed. The main thing is finding the right place for them, and making sure that they are fenced in properly, away from foxes and rats. It was funny, really because at the beginning I had got them so barricaded in, that I had forgotten to leave enough space for me to get to them.

'Just put two handfuls of the pellets in that tray please Lily.'

'Is that enough?'

'Perfect, they have two of those and they've still got some of the corn and potato peelings left so that should be enough. With the nights drawing in now, they'll soon be getting ready for bed time.'

'Do you put heating on for them?'

'Ah! Sweet, no Lily, they don't need electric blankets. They're feather downs themselves, so they keep snug on their own. The only thing in the winter is that they do poo a lot more because of the dark, and because the foxes are hungry, they are more at risk of being hunted down. I'll sweep it out early tomorrow morning, so if you hear me stirring early, just go back to sleep.'

'Goodness you have a busy life'.

'Do you think so? It's simple and I'm well occupied and it feels healthy. There are, let me hang up your fleece for you and you get by that fire now and have a warm up. I enjoy spending time outside, probably as much because I absolutely love coming inside afterwards.

Now it's Bumbles' turn. See, she's ready for a comb, very cooperative aren't you? There now. Look at all this fluff. It's very important if you have a dog like this to keep on top of his coat; the fluff goes in a paper bag like this, soft and downy and purely taken from the undercoat, only the best for spinning...I really love that, it's one of the most relaxing things to do.'

'Doesn't it make you sneeze?'

'Yes, sometimes, but it's not too bad because it is clean and washed before the spinning starts.

'It's so cosy here.'

'Well, the fires and stove make it like that. I can keep the stove in, most of the time in the winter, and just light the open fire sometimes. Now then, Bumbles that's you sorted. All our furry friends fed and seen to, it's our turn next: I'll pop our casserole in the oven now, it'll be done in an hour and three quarters.'

'Brilliant, well I'll go and make my phone call, have a rest and be downstairs by seven, if that's OK.'

'Of course, it is Lily; I'll probably nod off in the rocking chair myself for half an hour.'

By the time Lily came downstairs refreshed from her sleep, a cheerful fire had been re-lit in the front room and another peat log had been thrown on. Bumbles rose to her feet wagging her tail, and gave Lily a welcoming lick.

'She doesn't jump too high these days, hope you're hungry Lily?'

'That looks absolutely gorgeous. Did you make me nice things like that when I was little?'

'Shepherd's pie was one of your favourites. Even when you had birthday parties, you would ask for
'shep's pie please'. Do you remember much about it back there then?'

'Well, little bits I suppose. I remember that bucket chair in the kitchen, and sitting at the table with newspaper on it, painting. I remember that boy with the big fringe, the one that had the little brother who was a pain. He used to chase after me all the time and find things to poke me with; what were they called?'

'That was Matthew and I've forgotten his little brother's name, I didn't know he was like that! Do you remember anything about school? Mrs Pilkington was your teacher.'

'She was simply the best! Fleur enthused,

'She always wore bright necklaces. I wonder what they were really like? I just always think of her with that necklace. Fruit gums, that's what it reminded me of, but I can't really remember I just imagine the stones were like that. She smelt nice too. I remember always loving it when it was home time and you came to collect me and you never minded me having anyone come home, did you?'

'Would you prefer hot custard or single cream, or both?'

'Bit of both is definitely always welcome.'

'O go on, at least a thousand sentences ago you started to tell me about your dad and his Greek lady friend.'

'Olga? Yes, she's all right really,' she said with a catch of caution and sensitivity towards me in her voice.

'She has gorgeous long black hair, the kind with a natural curl. She likes to spend time with her family, and because there is the language problem, dad just lets her get on with it. Probably quite helpful really that there's a language barrier, puts less strain on my dad to communicate. There seems enough to interest them both. He loves Greek food but much of the daytime is spent in separate lives. He never talks about Uncle, or Mum. If I say anything at all, he cuts me dead. If he gets the smallest hint I am going to say something he steers the conversation away; gets on my nerves a bit sometimes the way he does that; I can't help mum being mum, or her having died the way she did, but it's even the same if you come up in conversation. Anyway, that's better than it used to be. When I was about fourteen, if anything came up then, he was so rude about you.'

'Never mind!' that was one of my father's phrases.'

'Never mind' can ease a lot of thoughts. Go on.' Lily was looking at me, and maybe sensing some kind of strain.

'Never mind, on the plus side I suppose although things are restricted between us, you know between dad and me, I'm lucky to have gone to a good school and I'm glad he's got Olga because I don't have to bother about him, he's looked after. I would have much preferred to have gone to a normal grammar school, but given our personal circumstances boarding really did help. Poor granny is alone now: old pops died three years ago, but he'd had a good long life.'

'O, I am so sorry.'

'It's ok, she's doing well, I think he'd become a bit hard work towards the end; she's a lot more rested now. She had no idea you'd moved to Devon, wait until I tell her what it's like: she'll be thrilled for you. I love the oak beams and 'bump your head ceilings!' and everything.

'However did you find me?'

'You might well ask. How many times have you moved?'

'You did take a bit of tracking down. I'm so pleased Aunty, it's so quaint. How did you end up here?'

'O, it was just one of those things really but would take me a few days to explain,' Lily laughed, in just the kind of knowing way her mother would have. How lovely it was to have this homely chat with her, after all this time.

Lily was soon telling me about Martin and all he meant to her; how they had met, what he looked like, how she felt she could be herself with him, the list of positives seemed endless, and then with clammy hands over mine, she paused and the phone rang. It was for her, and seeing the lift in her spirits as she greeted Martin, I popped into the kitchen to make us another drink; a welcome breather and give her some privacy. Lily had come home. For how long was of little concern - why now? I would gradually discover.

The next thing I knew Lily was curled up on the window seat, in reminiscing mode. She put another log on the burner, closed the door as the flames danced and conjured up increasingly thoughts for both of us. It was as if she had known the house and Bumbles a lifetime. They sat closely together, Lily fondling her most of the time as her stories emerged.

Lily had such a compelling sadness about her, an expression in her beautiful eyes and yet at this moment with the interruption from the telephone she was bubbling away again, and I was glad that that was happening.

The kitchen at the cottage was my favourite room, as it was cosy yet spacious enough for a wood burning stove and sitting area as well as the cooking activity and it felt so good to be able to talk, listen and cook at the same time. It became the room where Lily and I would sit around the stove chatting.

'So what did you do when you left school?'

'O, I went au pairing to two children in Richmond for a while; the eldest was aged four and the youngest was just two years six months: they were gorgeous, spoiled rotten but delightful too and that's where I met Rob.'

'Rob?'

'O, yes, sorry, Rob, he was real cool.'

'What happened to him then?'

'Don't you mean what happened to me?'

The kettle went on and soon she was telling me of past love tales: Rob had meant a lot to Lily clearly, and she was really sad when he finished with her. Lily filled up as she gave me snippets of the love she had felt for him, but ended with a typical Maria kind of jest,

'Anyway I certainly don't miss his smelly socks, and the way he never learned to put the loo seat down!'

'Bumbles doesn't seem to like the sound of that either, you know. Just look at her! 'And with that, Bumbles had slowly risen to her feet, shaken herself and flopped down again, this time by the fire, next to Boss and nearer to my feet.

'He was my first proper boyfriend,' Lily continued,

'You know what I mean? I had had sex before but with Rob it really meant something different, yes, so I grew up a lot with him.'

'So what happened then? Ok, not in too much detail!'

'I started a Tops secretarial course and did a course in modelling. So then, a series of 'no hopers' followed. Well that's not quite right really, I suppose, I was just discovering the company of men, and time just passed in a harmless kind of way. Poor Derek at the office, he was really nice and we would spend loads of time chatting, but'

'He was always about to leave his wife?'

'Yes, you're right how did you know?'

'Feminine intuition.'

'No, I knew several Dereks too; there are plenty around, but we don't have to be taken in by them do we?'

'Aunty Fleur!'

'O, Fleur please.'

'I had this image of a one man Aunty, never recovered from the loss of Uncle Jeremy and all the time she was a piranha on the quiet?'

'O, no darling, that's not true. Jeremy will always be the love of my life and for years after the tragedy it was like that but ..

'Go on you mean you've still got a bit of a Felicity Kendall look about you, I mean in the days when she was in the Good Life and all the men loved her.'

'O, I don't know about that, but anyway.'

We laughed our way and progressed to a bottle of wine, until we found ourselves crying our way through another one. Lily was concerned to make sure I understood that she had not had an affair with Derek, but he had always indicated he would like a relationship with her if only he could un-marry himself.

'I can see now, that was his 'give away' line. I should have seen it coming. What a waste of time!'

Lily told me about her broken engagement to Mark, all very traumatic to escape when a lakeside wedding had been arranged and guests invited and it was only six weeks before the wedding.'

'Six weeks?'

'Yes, so close to it, I started to feel uneasy about things. I felt really oppressed by his family - somehow they made me feel I might explode. He was okay really, but all of a sudden he wasn't on the pedestal where I had placed him, and I wanted to run away. More away from his family than from him, but I couldn't have one without the other. It was so difficult to put things into words; he hadn't done anything-wrong Fleur, he was still the same. My experience of it all had changed and here I was six weeks before the wedding having to call it all off and no doubt causing him lifelong stress and consequences as a result.'

'That was so brave of you; especially when arrangements need cancelling and you have to face all those people. I had a broken engagement to deal with but it was different because being older, there wasn't a fancy wedding arranged and in my case I didn't really face anything.'

'So what did you do?'

'I just ran away.'

All of a sudden emotion from way back came out in this 'at home' feeling that Lily had given me in her sweet unmeasured listening, where I felt she was freely happily with me for all the time in the world (even though I knew it would only be a day or two).

'Go, on, Aunty Fleur tell me about Cyril, it wasn't anything to do with his family, nothing like my situation it sounds. O, Aunty, I mean Fleur, I'm so sorry.'

'Well, before I get on to that, honestly I did have some really fun times and some lovely girlfriends and the moving around never bothered me.'

'Did you move a lot?'

'I suppose so, but it was relatively simple because I usually stayed in rented property: I wasn't buying houses or anything so I was just able to think after a while: 'time for another move!'

'But Fleur, it's one of the most stressful things moving.'

'Well, no, it wasn't to me, the change of scenery and the anonymity it afforded me felt so good, at least for a while; I felt a bit back in charge of my life again. I chose to settle wherever I was, for a while and took an interest in my surroundings and gradually getting to know a few people helped. I didn't want to be known as the lady who all those things happened to and so it took a while for me to find ways of talking to people where I could be friendly enough without having to get into a lot of those details.'

'I can see that.'

'And you're talking about twenty years or so since we had contact, and that's a lot of time. So I suppose my 'Rob' did you say Rob? Was 'Paul,' he was the one I should have married, if I was to take that step again; I knew it could never be like my marriage to Jeremy, nothing could begin to compare to that.'

'I know, but what was he like?'

'Very street-wise. He had been married twice before, divorced from both. At the beginning it felt strange meeting someone divorced, as if a widow should only really meet another widow, to be on the same wavelength. Yes, I think Paul really did love me and I believe I loved him. We sparked off each other's sense of humour really well and he seemed to value me for the person I am. He was medium height, lean and fit. He noticed small details in the way I do things that I suppose make me, me, and yet which I wasn't so conscious of. I felt approved of, loved and valued. He made me feel like a million dollars. I loved his command of language and his choice of words that came with ease and a natural poise. His being a journalist was fascinating to me.'

'Ah, he sounds charming, and you're from a similar background, with the librarian in you, love of books, so why did it change?'

'I suppose it was a mixture of things really. Nothing changed between us: it was a relationship that in a way had no end. He got a six months posting as foreign correspondent, which no doubt we could have coped with, and if push came to shove I could have moved with him, to a nearby location. But I suppose that side of me started a bit of a worrying train of thought in my mind, as it was important amidst excitement to also feel settled and safe. Occasionally, I would think, I wonder what his second wife would say about him. Had both the wives before felt so reassured at the beginning? Then whilst that was happening Marilyn rang.'
'Who's Marilyn?'
'Marilyn was a close friend of mine going back to teenage years, so yes, it was just one of those 'out of the blue' unexpected things.'
Marilyn rang me to tell me that she had bumped into Cyril Taylor, a pharmacist from Clitheroe. I remembered him as a man, balding a little, with nice wife, Maud. Well, Marilyn went on to tell me that Maud had died two years before from breast cancer and that Cyril had been mortified by her death and had become increasingly reclusive. So there you have it, I immediately started to empathise for his situation and somehow started to see it as far more sensible a situation for me to be in than living a whirlwind life with a foreign correspondent twice divorced. So ridiculous when I look back because even though I had come across an old love letter Paul had sent to his second wife, in which he was writing a lot of loving things, it still didn't mean that the words he said to me back there then couldn't be true, but at the time I allowed that to sway me into believing I'd be more secure to pursue Cyril, the widower.'

'So hold on, what happened to beautiful Paul?'

'O, I don't know really, as I said, we didn't finish with each other, I don't think we could have done that; we never seemed to ruffle each other the wrong way, but I suppose we just started to walk along different paths.

Little could Fleur have known that for years following his going away, Paul would see her smile, her white teeth, her long, long hair, recall the logs on the fire, the smell of clean washing drying over the clothes maiden, the smell of a cake cooking. He knew it was her loveliness and her sad story that had contributed to his not being more persistent that they be together. He had worried that the porcelain she was made from, that he loved so much would break into a million pieces with the pressures and risks of the travelling. He had not real-ised Fleur was strong: her cracking only appeared with cruelty and unkindness, in every other respect she showed robustness and resilience, which she hadn't had a chance to show him at the time. She was more like a smooth piece of turned wood that might feel and have the sheen of porcelain but have the sturdiness of wood.

Little could Fleur have known that Paul had quietly pursued what was happening to her from a distance and with the ut-termost discretion? How disappointed he was and devastated when he discovered she was engaged to someone he believed she could not have loved in the way she loved him.

'So, there I was, back in the North. Soon after Cyril and I had met, it was all fixed and settled. It seemed to make sense that Cyril and I got together: two lonely people who had an un-derstanding for each other's grief and losses. We didn't ex-pect to fall in love but weary of our lives, just thought not to be alone any more would be enough. We both were comfort-able, had been left at least with no financial worries, and that was a bit of an attraction really, not for the money per se, but because we were balanced that way. In many ways he seemed to tick the boxes, although deep down I knew from the start, he didn't really tick any of them.

I remember going back to Cyril's house, seeing all his clocks; he had seven.'
'Never! Did you say seven clocks? Did you not think that a bit indulgent?
'No, just the opposite, you see our grandmother Lillian loved clocks, and your mum and I loved staying with her, and helping to wind up the clocks was such a happy time. So, on the contrary I sort of took it as a sign that this was meant to be. Ludicrous isn't it? The way we come to these decisions, talking ourselves in and out of things. Yes it's a funny thing; that grandma and the way we were so happy at home with her, was probably one of the main contributory factors to my thinking I'd be all right becoming Cyril's wife. I had grown tired of being alone, wanted to feel more settled again. Cyril was so completely the opposite of Jeremy and I thought that to be another positive, as I wouldn't be comparing them all the time. So we became engaged on Valentine's Day.'
'So did you love him by then?'

'No, I never loved him Lily, but I thought I might grow fond of him; the truth was he nearly drove me mental. By the time we had been together for eighteen months, he had twenty-three clocks: grandfather, grandmother, you know the long case clocks? He had Westminster chime mantelpiece clocks etc. etc. etc. and the winding up time of them all was ritually done. Unfortunately they didn't all go off at the same time, so that I found my head almost preparing to vibrate on the hour, or I would make every excuse to escape when I could. Friends and his family would welcome me.
'My! Not a bit like Maud! Then there'd be an awkward pause, a smile but an edge of a disapproving tone, which meant to my ears, "we don't like you as much.'
'She must have been a bit mad don't you think?'
'No, she was probably just happily accepting. Maybe she loved his growing interest with the clocks and the security

and predictability he gave; her adoring very quiet unchallenging stance was what he felt relaxed with and maybe he became more obsessional after he had lost her. No, I think Maud was a dear person on all accounts. I just felt so oppressed by him and it made me miss Paul and your Uncle Jeremy so much. Do you know, Lily, there was a time when I would have given anything for Cyril to have an affair with someone? It would have given me a legitimate reason to leave him.

Sounds trivial doesn't it, but it was horrible'. I looked at Lily, and we hugged and hugged.

'So what happened in the end?'

'I planned it. Something terrible really; I deserted him.'

'Good for you'

'Well, it must have been awful for him to come home to my brief note.'

'Never mind him what about you?'

'I've never been back; everyone will have me down as the 'deserting cruel fiancée of the widower' maybe they wouldn't all think that, but I was fairly sure some would. I would be branded the heartless one.'

'I'm so sorry Fleur that you had all that.'

'Well, I don't want to go on about him to you Lily, I'm so sorry I didn't mean to be a burden to you but I did know I had to break free of him.'

'All those clocks, that's enough to drive anyone senseless. O, bless, I wish I had known, I'd have been there for you'. Lily with her reassuring tones went quiet.

'I'm just so sorry, as if you hadn't had enough heart-ache.'

'I know, but seriously, Lily, there have been many good, light times too. It's so important to remember that, when we hit the odd bad moment. I have made some really special friends, over the years, two or three really good girl friends who like me were on their own, and we had great times doing this and that together and having a laugh as we exchanged stories. So that's been a God send. Life's good a lot of the time isn't it?'

'I've brought a photo album with me, Fleur; my baby book. Would there be any chance of your explaining who's who in it? Dad was hopeless at that sort of thing until I realised he probably didn't know half the people. For ages I thought an old woman who appears in photos frequently with me, was my grandmother but then many years later I realised she was not Nana Elizabeth.'

'Ah! Lily, I know who that is, she's Annie. She was wonderful and a big part of my childhood as well as yours; she was married to Harry. They had two children: Susan and Billy.'

Gradually, I attempted to fill her in as best as I could, although no description of Annie could really do her justice. 'Heart of gold lady; I am so glad you have those pictures, Annie was a complete treasure, Lily.'

'O, yes that's June and Nick: he worked with your uncle and June was his wife. We used to go walking with them and during the time you and I were together, on our own, June would come swimming with us to give us a hand and sometimes we would go back to their house for tea and chocolate marshmallow biscuits! I wonder where they are these days.

That's Catherine and Tim. I worked at the library with Catherine and Tim was just brilliant. He used to ride you around on his shoulders.'

'Well, I have never seen that one before: your mother and father. Isn't that a lovely one?

'I love it, don't they look young? He looks like he is tickling mother.'

'Yes, he does.'

'And this one: they look like they've been on a long walk, don't they?

'Yes, they do.'

'Did she become poorly? Mum does look very pale, sad and thin in these later ones.'

'Yes, I can see what you mean, I think she wasn't always happy and that can make anyone look pale and pasty can't it?'

That night when I went to bed I said my prayers for Lily; it was just marvellous to see her after all this time. I worried a bit about my having told her that her mum wasn't always happy, but good that she also had some earlier happier photos to keep. Had I told her too much about Cyril and things? I consoled myself that there was a lot I had left unsaid, so I had been somewhat discerning. I might share more with her in time, but she had enough shocks/surprises with what I had told her. I had left unsaid how poorly I had been for a while, in mind and body; all the traumas of the accidents and the Alistair/ Cyril experience had brought the pins and needles of my life screaming back to me.

I didn't tell her how for a while the retreat at York became my home: it was my sanctuary and salvation. I didn't tell her how I learned so much there, in so many different ways, not just from the therapy, but from the space and safety around me, from the stories I was hearing from others, which every now and then helped to illuminate my own.

For the first time I was seeing how my immaturity and na-ivety combined with an overriding desire to please, placed me at high risk, in the wrong relationship of being fodder for the bullies of the world. I became weary of the things life had hurled at me. But I always responded so well to kindness shown.

It didn't feel like therapy, or that I was with 'mental health cases'. I was shocked at myself for even thinking like that. There was something about the atmosphere of 'acceptance' that made me feel at home. I made such good friends there, Sandy, Edna and Paula. It was real, in its unusual sort of way. We all knew we didn't have to keep meeting up again to know we were friends - our paths could just exist alongside each other in those moments. It was a sort of institution, but not a place to fear. It is ironic that whilst my background had perhaps not prepared me for some of the cruelty that can happen in life; back at the retreat in the world of therapy, we were all being given the kindness, help and sensitivity that had been home at Springhill.

I could smell the Retreat again, smell the newly cut grass outside, the polished banister in the welcoming hallway. I could see Hugh the gardener, who never said a lot but always had a smile and a warm exchange with you and realized that in a very similar way I was recalling Springhill again, and celebrating so much of it in a new way. It was at the Retreat, where, after a while (probably only two months that felt like an eternity) I started to remember lots and lots of the good things in life; the walks, the places and faces.

I could cope again with memories of home and the fundamental hard work, love, fun and artistic stimulation that was there. It was how to deal with conflict that I had had to awaken to in adulthood, something that we had had little experience of at home. It was such a wonderful feeling to get back to, but to be making sense of the wider picture in a way that might bring me more peace and balance.
I went asleep thinking of Sandy and Paula again wondering where they were, what they were doing these days. I found it hard to imagine they were getting older now like me.

'Did you sleep well Fleur? Here you are! I reckoned it might be nice for you to have breakfast cooked for you for a change.'
'That's gorgeous, Lily, and you've lit a fire too, bless you.'

A lovely day followed where we had lots of light moments: hugs, a bit of walking, talking, shopping, a bit of television, and then we were back to some deeper sharing in the evening.

'I'm so glad you told me about Cyril, must have been so hard, but sounds like a lucky escape.'

'I was just thinking though Lily. I was lucky in some ways. It was invaluable to have had that training as a librarian because I was never short of work and many of the skills were transferable to other things so that was good too. I was lucky with those girlfriends I was telling you about. One of them was called Gemma and she had roots in Devon. Amidst Gemma's stories were wonderful descriptions of Devon and Cornwall, the hedgerows, the primroses, countryside that rolled along to the sea. She would tell me about her growing up and holidaying in Cornwall and the east coast of Devon. It was on one of those lazy evenings dreaming where we were in life and where we'd all be in five years' time that lead me to think somewhere like East Budleigh, could be a lovely place to be for a while. Gemma was going to stay with her aunt for a month and I decided to take the train, have a break and call on her and the rest is history. It was one of those golden moments, stumbling on this cottage, a stroke of luck. I love being here, watching the waves, the watery reflections in every piece of glass and art that you see.'

'I'm so glad for you aunty.'

'And your being here is the icing on the cake.'

Polly loved East Devon, and was so glad the book took her back there.

Another evening rolled by and Lily was looking more rested. Little by little she explained that she had been advised to seek rest by the doctors. Martin and she had had the sadness of a stillborn baby. The baby, a boy was born full term with congenital leukaemia. It had come as such a shock and they really mourned the little boy. Congenital leukaemia is a rare condition to lead to a stillbirth and of course Lily knew about Christopher so the genetic counsellor was trying to fill in the family history with them to weigh up risks etc. for the future.

I could see the sadness in Lily's eyes, the disappointment and anxieties.

'I felt shocked by my own body, isn't that awful Fleur, but I did. I had given birth to something that wasn't right and, what's more, had been invisibly carrying this around with me for nearly a year without knowing. It was only momentary that I had that awful thought but I did. It really was so sad Aunty. Giving birth is so incredibly difficult once you know you've lost the baby, it's like having to part with something on one level you don't want to part with, and then there's all the pain of child birth on top, and I had no mum to talk to.'

'O, Lily, I am so sorry.'

'It's all right; I am okay most of the time. I can think of him now as my little angel, there are even days when I imagine how old he is and think what he would look like. It's just I know Martin wants a family and I am failing him already.'

'Darling, has he said that?'

'No.'

'He adores you and this baby belonged to the two of you didn't it?'

'Yes.'

'Well then.'

'Yes, but I mean it's from my side isn't it? I always knew about Christopher so that's it.'

'Now hold on, I don't know enough about all of that side of things. You are both grieving. I know from the way that phone rings with calls from Martin from all over the place one thing is certain, he loves you to bits, doesn't he? Even if there is a genetic link to our family you need not think of it in terms of blame.'

Lily was in my arms wetting the collar of my blouse with her tears as she nodded and cooed about the way Martin showed her so much love.

'Do you know Fleur, some days, even seeing a lot of people in a shop can feel too much and I even find raised voices or anything like that gets to me. Some days even answering the phone feels too much. I thought I knew what some of the future was going to bring: a family and now everything's different. It's like if I take that brave step to get pregnant, no matter how much the genetic counsellor advises me I can predict just how on edge we're both likely to be; it makes me feel almost sick thinking about it and I never was one for wrapping myself up in cotton wool; yet this is what I feel like I'm inclined to do these days. Say something, please, what's wrong?'

'O, it's all right dear. I was just thinking of how we all are so programmed to expect everything always to be perfect; a life is a life and everyone who tries for a baby carries some risks. We carry risks when we wake up each morning and know we have roads to cross.'

All I could do was comfort her and I was wondering how much more Maria might have done for her. She knew the pain and anticipation of having a child.

'I wish I could help more, Lily. It might not be much consolation because I know it's different, but believe me I do know how frightening it can be to feel so very fragile at times.'

'You are helping me already, Fleur, more than you could ever know'. I took Lily a warm drink to her bedside and then stayed up a bit longer.
That night my bed felt so empty again. Lily and Martin had had such a shock; they would have been good parents to the little child and will have felt the loss so much.

Like putting the clocks back I was remembering the days and months following our marriage when Jeremy and I were hoping for our family. We thought it would come so easily. Little by little the light of day dawned with us and it was a harsh reality to take and became so hard to talk about. It was if 'the world and his wife' were having babies and would naturally be full of baby talk and either seem insensitive to us or over sensitive: the truth was no one could really get it right for us because there was no getting it right. Eventually we came through it all and knew we would have to accept our situation and take it from there.

I felt sad and angry for Lily; it didn't seem to be fair. How tragic for them to have had a stillborn baby and now have to be facing further dilemmas - but they would get through. How strange in a way that eventually I had that chance to bring baby Lily up for five years. With that thought I gradually fell asleep, remembering Lily's rosy soft cheek on mine, the way she used to whisper things to me so that no one else would hear even though we were there on our own. I started to remember Lily like it was yesterday; Mat, Helen and Daisy from play school days were her special friends and would come to our house to play. I used to love to see them sitting round the table having sandwiches and a piece of fruit, chatting and giggling together. I was glad Lily remembered them.

C14:   Portrait of a lady

The phone rang, and half an hour later I was knocking at the
door of Father Tim. Lily stayed at home to rest.
'Come in, my dear,' he said as he saw the tiredness on my
face. He was brilliant like that. I could be myself with him
because no matter how I was, our boundaries were clear and
he always knew I was of good intention. His way was simple
with me, he accepted me the way I was. I blurted out my di-
lemma, the one Lily had told me.

After a pause, he told me that sometimes he believed one
thing could be answered, indirectly, by helping someone to
see a story within a story like the Russian dolls that hold one
inside another inside another inside another, so that it becomes impossible to tell where one story starts and another
ends. It felt such a relief to be in his loving and honest company. He asked if I would go into the parlour to see a friend
of his who may need me.

I pushed open the parlour door. In the far corner of the room
was an elderly priest with white hair. His face was like a
book: wizened with age but it had the depth that made you
want to keep turning pages. He looked pale and troubled. On
the wall over the fireplace was a portrait of a beautiful woman. The priest explained his mind had been troubled all of his
life, but now he felt so pleased to be meeting Father Tim's
friend, he had heard a lot about me and was needing to talk.

'Could there be a place just sometimes for space for confession, not from a priest but from the man who had become a
priest all those years ago, someone who had known pain and
sadness?' His request was so gentle and fragile.
'I am here' I said, sensing this was the way that Father Tim
wished me to help: he wanted me simply to listen. 'Please, I
will listen.' At that he smiled.

'A long time ago I had a small parish in the highlands of
Scotland. I had spent years at the neighbouring seminary, but

O, my child, how guilty I feel with hindsight. I should have married Elise. That's Elise, the lady in the portrait. If I had done so, she may not have died.' He continued to tell me that the lady had always lived a removed, sheltered life for reasons best known to herself. He discovered after she died that her young French husband was killed in the war, only five weeks after they had been married. She never recovered from this traumatic experience, so dedicated her life to quietly helping others.

'Of extraordinary beauty inside and out she, could almost have been a nun herself, the way she lived her life; she was both spiritual and a very musical person and lived in the annex by the nuns because she helped out with some teaching. I too had association with the convent at that time, so that was how we met. I hope I am not embarrassing you, opening up like this, but I feel sure you will understand how an old man towards the end of his life might have this need to talk. One day, Elise and I by chance were sitting next to each other at the same chamber music concert; Debussy Le prelude d'un faun d'apres midi. We sat quietly and excitedly moved, in awe of the music of its power and sensitivity. It felt almost 'meant to be'; as if some invisible hand had guided us to know each other better, through that amazing concert. We became the best of friends thereafter and we met regularly over several intense weeks.'

'As a young man, on the brink of deciding whether to become a priest, I was somewhat preoccupied, still in a state of indecision about my future. One part of me thought I had a calling to the priesthood; another part of me thought it might be a calling to be a family man. In meeting Elise my thoughts kept fluctuating and, six months before joining the seminary, I found myself relaxing, allowing myself to be fascinated by Elise and falling in love with her whilst she seemed to have found in me someone too she could really trust, who would really listen to her. She too was, I think, falling in love with me. It was as if we had found in each other the kind of soul mate that meant you could really speak your heart out without having to put anything through any kind of sieve in your head leaving out bits that might shock or hurt. We were able to say anything to each other, and in this process we started to see ourselves more clearly.'

'Gradually Elise started to reveal her emotional trauma.' He sighed and continued.
'Something dreadful happened,' which was why she had to hide away. The secret? She had a child, out of wedlock, with a man she hardly knew.'
'How sad,' I said as I looked at the tenderness in her face.
'Indeed, and there's more,' continued the priest, who went on to tell Elise's story.
'The guilt and shame weighed so heavily on her shoulders. What would she say to people?
What would people think of her? It was so out of character, yet it had happened. What would she say to the child about the father? Somehow she got through the pregnancy but her torture was exhausting to her and she had the child, a little girl. She was eternally grateful to one of her friends, a nun at the convent, who promised to help her. She had experience of helping to raise a number of wartime babies and would be an everlasting support.

Gradually we fell in love, but never verbalised it to each other. We couldn't. Elise worried she would be offending me, after all she knew I had ideas of being a priest; I worried I might be offending her, because she had experienced such sorrow and abuse. It was a relief for her that I knew of her little daughter. However after one night of excessive reflection and intensity, I suppose the inevitable happened; I took Elise into my arms, we made our feelings known to each other in an act of real love.

Believe me, it was the only experience of loving this way that I had ever had and remained so for the rest of my life. Forgive me, perhaps for speaking of it now, but why not. Some sins have long shadows. If only we could have talked to each other about it. Making love that one night had changed everything and left us speechless; what to do next? We had both come to that place we can sometimes experience in life where for some reason we find ourselves truly lost, as we step into the unknown, a place of no return. I wondered if she thought she had been betrayed, that someone else had taken advantage. I looked at her.

She looked like a painting, in a way that could render a man speechless. I thought we had time to talk.
I left her to rest.
I walked the dog. I came home.
She was gone.
She left me a note saying:

Sometimes the right words are difficult to find, they travel a long way back in your heart. Some relationships never really end...
Elise.

Tears were rolling down the old man's face. I held his hand and spoke to him with my eyes.
'At that time, I chose to see her going away as a rejection of a kind, of me. No, I did not choose to see it that way, then, I just simply did not see another way to think. Now, with the benefit of hindsight, I believe, she was giving me a gift: the gift of space. She could not decide for me, whether I was to be priest or husband; her presence would only keep on influencing me, and that would be too big a burden for her, or rather should be my burden, not hers. I knew not where she went, or what happened to her, but I always remembered.
I went on to be a priest and as I took my vows I thought I could see her smile in approval of the vocation I would be following.

Many years later, I heard from a mutual friend of ours that Elise had died. She had died soon after giving birth to a little daughter, who she called Fleur. How I wish I had asked her to marry me and perhaps if I had done so, she would not have had all the heart ache that lead to her death.'
'What happened to Fleur?' I asked with tears in my eyes.

'Elise had seen to everything. She had asked the Sisters that should anything ever happen to her, would they please look after the girls until they found a good loving couple to raise them. She was not morbid about this but did have a feeling always, that she might die young.'
'Have you heard of a heart breaking, I mean really breaking?' The priest went on, 'I kept looking forward.

'After a while, I went just the once to see Sister Bernadette. She made no overt connection to me, but looking downwards, told me she knew Elise was really in love with the father of this little girl. I could hardly contain the moment I saw the most beautiful little girl in the world, the miracle of life. I could see Elise in her and was left wondering the rest. I had been too proud to follow things through and find out what had happened, and the not knowing now is a torture beyond belief.'

'Stop now please,' I interrupted, with a silencing gesture.
'I think if I were the little girl, the daughter of your beautiful friend, I would understand. Isn't it the most natural thing in the world that you spent time 'wondering' what life would have been like had you married Elise? But none of us know what would have happened do we? Did you ever stop to think, she might have said 'No', and married someone else or she might have died anyway. How often we fill in, torture ourselves, imagining how if such and such had happened it would all have been different when even with those differences things may have worked out differently than expected.

The old priest's eyes were listening intently and as he spoke, his voice sounding increasingly frail.

'The nuns looked after Elise's two little girls until one day they heard of the dreadful grief of a doctor and his wife who had lost their son.'

'Thanks be to God'. I was so relieved to hear the calm of another priest's voice taking over.

'You have truly given so much, Father, sacrificed things and been devoted in your ministry. We know not the order of events, in life and God's plan for us.

Go in peace now

And let perpetual light shine upon him'

I could only faintly hear the priest completing a prayer at my side as the dear old priest more connected to me than I could have known was laid to rest. I knelt quietly beside him and prayed, as I looked upward to the portrait of Elise, my mother.

My heart was racing:

I thought of mother and father, how we loved them.

I thought of the letter re: wanting to see the two of us on our own.

Was this secret the thing, they were going to tell us at their ruby wedding? I had just seen my mother, a portrait of her on the wall and maybe I had come face to face with my father? Of that I would never be sure. What I did know was that the person who I had just seen, had at one time been very close to my mother and that felt of significance to me, and I had just seen him die.

I rushed out of the church for some air, my asthma calling me. I needed to anchor myself; I was full of the pain of the priest and Elise: our real mother; the beauty and tragedy of it all. I went back inside and into the chapel leaving a burning trail of candles by the statue, and in that flickering moment, I reached to the things I knew: our good parents, and Springhill. I could almost hear our parents say:

'So now you have it, the missing pieces of the jigsaw' I thought of their sad loss, of Christopher and all those visits to the convent.

'If only I could bring them back and have a conversation, a hug with them now.'
'To everything, turn, turn, turn, there is a season, and a time for every purpose under Heaven,' echoed in my ears. When would it ever have been the right time to tell us?

Polly was sobbing –

I remembered how the little niece Lily who had lost so much was constantly loved and cared for by myself, Annie, her paternal grandparents. There was a whole gap of time that I knew little about.
I remembered that Lily like another Fleur was back home now worrying over the 'should I, shouldn't I,' decisions of life. All of a sudden it became clear. I simply needed to be with her now, rather than in my head puzzling.

Lily needed me. I rushed home excited, and exhausted. When would I tell her about her mother and me? Would it make any difference to Lily and Martin for the future? We can only do the best at the time we are in, and then all the 'ifs,' in the world can only be swept to the side to rest.

Before telling Lily anything I felt I needed time with Sister Bernadette. I pictured her now as if she was holding a giant sized key. I thought of our regular visits to the convent. I thought of darling Maria, Jeremy, mother and father, the old priest.
I thought of the portrait of the beautiful lady, mother of Maria and myself. I remembered how we had always been likened to the Dr and Elizabeth, and how like them also, we were and yet we weren't related. I thought my head and heart were going to burst....

By some miracle I managed to see dear old Sister Bernadette just before she died. How brave she had been to sustain so much in her mind for so long. How much of all of this would I share with Lily now?

In my mind, I held Lily in my arms and hugged and hugged her. Could she cope hearing all of this, when she was full up with thoughts of babies and so many other things. One step at a time; we would all cope; there had been plenty of steps before us.

Tears rolled down Polly's cheeks.

C15: The green door of home

It was now the early hours of the morning. By 7am, I heard Lily stirring and as she came downstairs into the kitchen. I held her in my arms and hugged and hugged her. Lily told me she would be leaving later that afternoon, but would return again within three months.

Just before leaving, Lily turned to me, in the morning light and unexpectedly said;
'Just one thing, Aunty Fleur, I have been thinking: why did my dad force me away from you so abruptly?'
I wasn't prepared for this, not at that moment with so much more to think about.
I hesitated before selecting to tell her that it would always have been an emotional moment but we would talk more another time.
'He's not so bad these days,' Lily added, as if in tune with the past.
'I still have difficulty trusting him, but Martin says that's ok. Its 'cause of losing mum and our unsettled beginnings which meant I didn't get to know dad till later, and then I never had a proper chance, because he was with someone else, and I was away at school, and parted from you: all a bit of a mess really; I just wondered why it had been decided I had to go back to him.'

I didn't reply. I told Lily that I would come and see her and Martin together soon, and also that I would research some information for them on the genetic side of things.

Weeks passed. We met up happily. It was great to meet Martin and it had been useful to have had that bit of space. They looked so right for each other; the flat was bright and cheerful and they were pleased to see me and have me visit their home. They soon introduced me to Dusty, the little kitten they had adopted from the cat's litter next door. Eventually I told them I had discovered that Christopher was not the brother of Maria and me, although we had always thought so. I explained further that Maria and I were sisters but that the wonderful thing was I had just learned that Grandma and Grandpa Andrews had adopted us both, all those years ago following their sorrow at the loss of Christopher. Wide-eyed, Lily squealed with delight and hugged me. She told me she had sometimes had fantasies about who she was herself.

'It was all jumbled up; I would wish you were my mum sometimes or think that I was a princess who had been adopted. I used to think my dad was not my dad at all. How amazing and then you tell me this!'

'What a relief,' I thought, 'I couldn't have predicted a reaction like that.'

'Grandma Elizabeth and Grandpa Andrews; weren't they fantastic!
I'm so glad I have this photo. I would have loved to know them. I must put it in a frame. Brilliant! Tell you what, that's what we might do if we have any more problems baby wise. We'd adopt wouldn't we Martin?'

How amazing that Lily's first reaction was like this after all my agonising. With this came another turning point.

From then on I vowed to live my life in cameos of time with boundaries, but without so much fear, and anticipation of things being too much. It wouldn't be, because it would simply be one of the cameos.

Thinking in cameos of time helped Fleur no end, and Lily too, but first Fleur had to come to terms with her struggles with Alistair. She knew she could never prepare herself for the moment when she heard more about him from Lily (who had grown to have a slightly strengthened relationship with him as time went by). The most Fleur could do was give Lily the space to do whatever she had to do, and Fleur?

She allowed herself to settle to her position of not taxing herself with too much new exposure and expectations to be meeting Alistair, because of Lily's renewed connection with her. He was 'the cloud in the silver lining,' she really searched her conscience about this, but the way Fleur settled her mind about these steps, was to think that Lily had come back into her life as an adult and that was a wonderful thing. Alistair, as far as Fleur was concerned, had to belong to her past. She knew she had soul searched in many different ways, but eventually with everything that had happened something had snapped inside her, that for her 'forever more' was her distance regulator.

It was an emotional evening when Fleur, settling by a roaring fire, took the further step of talking to Lily. She would never know the courage it took to do so. Fleur knew it might compromise their own relationship; she did not wish to make things more complicated for Lily or cause her disappointment. Nor did she wish Alistair any harm. However, Fleur also felt that in being as honest as she could be with herself, she was perhaps making it easier in the long run. She never wanted to create a 'you choose him or me' situation. Lily could have both of us but separately.

I told Lily what I felt I could about the long-term difficult relationship between her dad and Jeremy, and how the situation was made so much more complex by the fact that the two brothers had married two sisters. This was as much as I felt I could start to give as any kind of explanation for my saying 'please accept to keep me away from meetings with your father.'

I explained that rather than thinking of it as avoiding things, I now needed the assurance of some peace from the pile up of too many memories from things that might remain too much for me. Although I left a lot unsaid, what I did say flowed naturally, as I really felt her listening to me. I am not sure how I went on to explain things but I did get across to her that I was sorry for a layer of complexity all this inadvertently might be putting on to her but it was the most honest way forward that I could find and with my life nearly over that was all I felt I could do.

For where does a story start? How can you know the end when the beginning doesn't really exist either, because isn't the beginning of one thing the end of another? And increasingly layers that happen add to and take away from the original picture.

The expression in Lily's eyes touched my heart even though I knew I had left some things unsaid for now.

Was she being selfish? Not being able to put everything behind her? Being seen not to be able to let go? Some might say so, but whilst she continued to care for people and their feelings, she had reached the point where she felt less ruled by what the 'imaginary 'they' would think. What would the Retreat think? She would often lean on this way of thinking in helping her to make her mind up about anything.

Fleur chose to believe that the Retreat would shed their light and only tell her how brave she was being to find this new honesty in herself. It was not emotional blackmail. Some of the things could die with her some day, but meanwhile she knew she could only be as sincere as possible to herself as well as to others, in the shoes she was standing in. These days she knew she was able to see beyond people who might hint that she was being hysterical and know how she had held back so much for so long; she was far, far from being hysterical, and it had not been a dream. Maria and Jeremy's deaths were wrapped up in a dreadful nightmare of circumstances difficult for anyone to recover from. There might still be some tensions in the future but it was as far as everyone could go, as they all took their steps from their own shoes. I remembered Zac's words of wisdom in the group;

'Say nothing of me till you've walked a mile in my moccasins.'

'Lily love. Come and see,' Fleur had opened the back door into the night air. 'Look for that moon, how it's lighting the sky. It's the same moon your mum and I saw all those years ago, and it'll be the same one in years to come, that will be there when you choose to find it.'

I said no more but with excited reassuring eyes Martin and Lily had an idea of what I meant.

As time goes on I become more involved in helping at church: the youth group and the sick, and meet all sorts of people. I put this work alongside several other temping jobs which gives me variety and keeps me moving, learning and adapting to differences that are required, whilst it provides that structure you always told me about, and another thing: I never stop marvelling at what you used to say, how we all have the chance to learn something new each day.'

Extract taken from one of the last letters Lily wrote to Fleur before Fleur's death in 2005.

It was 13.12.2005, one of those crisp frosty mornings, when the phone rang with the wonderful news a little son was born to Lily and Martin; they called the baby: David Martin.

Bring Down the Moon

EPILOGUE. O' MOON SO BRIGHT

The book had sent Polly quivering, but somehow it felt personal and too near the surface to withstand having any kind of post mortem. Polly decided she would tell Sandra she had enjoyed it; she would reassure her that she would be thinking about what to do with it.

Polly felt she was still on a journey having read the story...a journey she didn't want to give up. She felt the power of the moon and found herself often strolling out into the night air, having a quiet think. Polly could be quite good at decision-making. She could sometimes detach herself from emotions if she was required to be in management mode. She decided she could think of this as a little project. There was no hurry, she could try to find out if there was a Springhill, a Fleur, a Maria, and if so could she find Lily?

Summer 2011
Polly found Springhill, and she found a parish magazine with reference to the doctor and his wife. A chance meeting with a woman who turned out to be Annie's daughter lead her straight to the library Fleur had worked at before the move to Devon. This in turn led to a forwarding address and here she was outside Number 8, Lily's house.

How would Polly explain herself? She took another look at it, as she did the cover. How would it piece together with the rest of Lily's life? Would it be welcomed or open a can of worms best left closed? Sitting in the car outside the door Polly pondered.

'What would Fleur want me to do?' The light was on in the sitting room and Polly could just make out the silhouette of a tall slender woman bending down to pick up a small child. **She looked up; the moon was once more over the doorstep as she stepped out of the car, and paused by the gate.**

Bring Down the Moon

Notes for Reading Groups

When we read, are we ever far away from our own stories?

Here are some guided reflections for *Bring Down the Moon* whether you are reflecting quietly on your own or in a reading group. It is not an English Lesson, but helps to place you (firmly) within your reading experience.

.

What is Biblio-therapy?

It is a way of reading literature in such a way that we give ourselves a chance to think of our own lives. Reading aloud or reflecting together is an interactive process and allows for different perspectives, creating fresh opportunities for freeing some of our stuck and limited thinking.

The notes set out are simply there to dip in and out of as you wish, not to be meticulously answered but to encourage conversation and reflections, and see where they take us with our own stories.

Perhaps reading will unearth a few cobwebs! Most of us have them: small regrets or things we wish might have turned out differently.

This is a technique that can be helpful when thinking of different characters, or people we know:

THUMB NAIL SKETCH TECHNIQUE

This is a way of drawing up a character. For example: Polly. Always think in 'I' terms.

'I am Polly. I work in a Charity Shop. My husband has died. I am efficient and warm, but enjoy being busy.'

You will each have your own unique spin on every character-that's what makes reading so fantastic. It's a chance to transport you out of yourself.

2nd **thoughts.** You can have lots and lots of second chance thoughts with the characters. You might feel angry with the character one minute, sad the next. It's OK

Chapter 1

Reflection 1   The birth of David Martin.

a)   **Read Aloud** those first few pages.
         Stay with the thoughts from the reading. You might want to close your eyes one moment, taking a breath in and out, and see the word in the air RELAX.

b)   **'How could she ever explain to Martin the mixture of emotion she was feeling: so, so happy, relieved and sad'**

         Mixtures of emotion can be hard to handle, any sharing?

c)   Lily's diary. How do you keep memories? Have you any letters squirreled away from the past. Do you take comfort from them?

f)   Anyone know the day they were born and in relation to the Monday's child poem. We only know what others tell us about our birth.

Reflection 2   Polly's Story

a)   Finding things can be fun. Have you ever stumbled on something special that has really gripped your attention?

Reflection 3   **Annie and Harry's story**

a)   **Annie.**

Do you know anyone like Annie? Just think about her a while and what she is saying to us in the story, the way she is an earth mother, and think of how you are. Another thought might be to wonder if there is anyone else who reminds you of an earth mother kind of person.

b)   **Harry.**

How are you drawn to him? What does his humour lend to the story? What do you think of them as a couple?

Exercise.   If Annie and Harry were in the group now:

a)   What would you want to say to them, or ask them?

b)   Would you want to see them together or on their own?

This is my life.

a)   Do Annie and Harry have a way of working things out that we might all learn from?

FAMILY SCRIPTS ref John Byng Hall

'All the world's a stage.'
The Family Script is a useful concept to grasp and can be very illuminating. You might want to look up about it. In a nutshell, we all have developed ways of doing things that we almost take for granted, but that routinely happen in our families, and once that happens and there's a sort of un-spoken script, then any departure from that might be seen as being 'not normal.'

Our corrective script is where we want to actively change something that we didn't like ourselves, for example Annie may have not liked having piano lessons as a child, so might decide when she has children that they won't be forced to play the piano. Think of aspects of your own corrective scripts and share.

How is Harry a big part of Annie's corrective script?

Reflection 4   **Dr. and Elizabeth returning home.**

a) **The loss of a child is profound**, and in the story connects in Annie's mind with her still born child and miscarriages. These personal experiences can be so difficult to speak up about. Perhaps this part of the story really resonated with some of us?

b) Perhaps in pairs we can think of a 'too much' feeling? Have you ever gone away to get away?

c) What touches does Harry bring to the grief picture?

d) How does the preparation Annie and Harry are doing uplift the anticipation of the homecoming?

'The moon was once more over their doorstep'

How does this reoccurring phrase in Bring Down the Moon, draw you in?

What does it mean to you? Has anyone close to you used any expression similar to that? For example: ' If I could bring down the moon for you I would.'

Chapter 2

Reflection 1   Polly

a) The plan for Polly changes. Would you go somewhere for lunch on your own?

b) How hard is it to get time for yourself?

Reflection 2   Mobile Phones
a) Polly switches her phone off. Perhaps it's an idea to think of life before mobile phones and the pluses and minuses associated with them.

Reflection 3   Silver Linings
a) Every cloud has a silver lining. Perhaps thinking in proverbs helps at times.?
Wonder what a silver lining day might look like?

b) How did Polly turn her disappointment at not meeting her friend into a silver lining? How does she keep things simple?

Reflection 4   What I did instead

a) Do you have contingency plans sometimes?

b) How spontaneous are you?

Reflection 5   **Springhill**

Springhill was 'home' to the girls, did you find yourself thinking of yours, or maybe someone-else you knew?

Reflection 6   **Grandparents**

a) How important were grandparents to you? Do you remember the loss of a grandparent? Polly had a good relationship with her grand dad, and the girls, never knew theirs.

If Only Exercise

Do you have an 'If only.' Most of our 'If Only' scenarios imply that everything would have been all right 'if only.' This feeds into negative circular spirals that further limit our thinking. The reality is that whilst we can have our 'if only' it is impossible to say what the outcome would have been. So, when we find ourselves thinking like this, perhaps we need to be realistic and add on, 'maybe it would have happened, or maybe not!'

a)   Do you remember your adolescence?

Reflection 7   **Angela's Family**

a) What does Angela bring to the story?

b) What stories do you remember of overnight stays?

Reflection 8   **'What I did instead?'**

a) Does Polly's train journey get you thinking?

Chapter 3

Reflection 1   **Polly's Journey**

a)   If you were to have a 'Penzance' place where would it be? Think of something you would love to have as a regular thing to look forward to 'doing.' How would it help you feel secure?

Reflection 2   **Maria's homecoming**

   a)   The story reconnects with the grown up sisters- they are very close. Did it make you think of anything?

   b)   How does the description of the 'bed-making' scene humour us back to the girls' relationship?

Reflection 3   **Fleur at the Library**

   a)   How does Fleur at the library link with the past and present?

   b)   Do you remember the library in those times?

Reflection 4   **Allan**

    a)   We learn of Fleur's early courting days. Did this part re-kindle any memories for you?

    b)   Do you ever wonder if someone from your past thinks of you?

Reflection 5   **Fleur's coming of age.**

    a) 21st celebrations used to be the big event, remember?

    b)   What do you think coming of age meant in the 60's?

    c)   What does the key to the door mean to you?

Reflection 6   **Two sisters marrying two brothers**

    a)   What do you make of this storyline?

    b)   Jeremy and Fleur love each other and couldn't have known then that Maria and Alistair would get together- has anything happened to you where an unexpected event made things so much more complicated for you?

Reflection 7   **Wedding bells**

    a)   Have you a rocking chair, or favorite chair that means 'home' to you?

    b)   Have you ever been in a situation like Fleur with divided loyalties?

Reflection 8   **Mr. and Mrs.**

a)   Being married makes a massive difference to the girls.

b)   Nowadays lots of people live together first. How might this be different?

Gavin and Elizabeth in planning their party ask for a **'happy and peaceful'** moment. What does this make us think about and how does the phrase start to take hold with us?

a)   The knock at the door: the police. How did you feel about this part of the story? Knocks at the door can mean all sorts of different things.

c)   The funeral: what did you make of this part of the story? Have you ever thought of your own?

Chapter 4

Reflection 1 **Polly and Bob.**

We hear about Bob. Does this come as a surprise to you? Does Polly help you think of your life?

Reflection 2 **Abuse of Maria**

a) Maria is in a cupboard under the stairs. How does this make you feel?

b) Can there be ways out of traps?

c) Sometimes just being aware of situations like that that can happen and be difficult to talk about might be worth considering.

Reflection 3 **Birth of Lily**

a) After the abuse of Maria we have the birth of Lily. Is that difficult to hear?

Reflection 4 **The scene in the car. Did it get you thinking of anything?**

a) The Trauma,. How did the description of it rest with you?

b) Did you start to think of your own life?

Reflection 5   **Facing difficult situations.**

    a)   Facing Alistair. We all know situations that are difficult to face.
Think of a situation you didn't want to confront, and see how it eventually was sorted or not.

Reflection 6   **Coping with Loss**

There has been a lot of loss in the story and different kinds of losses.

    a)   ' I'd Pick more daisies' Think of a daisy chain moment for yourself, and maybe share a loss or two.

Reflection 7   **Celebrating the moon and the stars.**

    a)   How liberating was this moment in the story: delighting in things that would still be there tomorrow?

Chapter 5   **The whole world had grown**

Reflection1   Portrait of Lily
          a)   Fleur in Devon: how much does it seem a new beginning?
          b)   How does Lily help to bring back Maria to us?

Reflection 2   **Filling in the Past**

          a)   Fleur starts to tell Lily things.
               Perhaps it reminded you of some situation of your own?

          b)   How much was it a shock to hear of Fleur's breakdown?

Reflection 3   **Fleur and Devon.**

          a)   What does this interlude bring?

          b)   What does Devon mean to you?

          c)   If you were to have a fresh start, where might it be?

          d)   How do the animals bring softness to the picture and are they important to you in your life?

Reflection 4   **'Part of me left the unexplained unheard and remained listening, for part of her was part of him and I was not in her shoes.'**

a)   What do you understand by this? Do we ever stand in another's shoes?

Reflection 5   **Priest House**

We see Fleur knock at the priest's door. At last she's going for a breather for herself.

a) The old priest starts to tell his story. As the story emerges, and we hear more of Elise, look at the words chosen to describe her and think of Fleur hearing those words and keeping her composure.

b) Have you ever gone to a friend wanting to talk about something, and instead end up listening to their problems?

Reflection 6   **Who do you think you are?**

a) Have you ever heard gossip about yourself?

b) Have you ever joined in one way whilst thinking another?

Reflection7   **Remembering her childhood.**

a)   Fleur is very selective in what she tells Lily. Discuss.

Reflection 8   **Cameos of time**

a)   What do Cameos of time mean to you?

b)   How might the idea help you?

Reflection 9   **Sister Bernadette, Gavin and Elizabeth**

a)   How did you like the image of Sister Bernadette holding a giant key?

Reflection 10   **Polly discovers Lily's address**

a)   Will she walk up the garden path?

b)   What would you do?

Where does a story start? Discuss what this means…

Thank you for reading and for travelling with Polly.

Notes for trainees

Using a narrative as an adjunct to course material can be a useful way of getting more practice from role-play and improvisation. You'll have a chance to get to know characters like Annie and Harry, Polly, Fleur and Maria and think into their shoes. This then becomes a rich resource for any role-play and improvisation, as it will feel 'so real.'

Chapter 1

1. **Life Cycle.**   The birth of David Martin:
    'I felt so so happy, relieved and sad.'

    Attachment theory.

    a) In pairs: share an attachment story you are familiar with personally, and think of the impact those first few moments had on later developments?

    b) Lily finds herself crying, whilst Martin is there but the feelings come out more when he has gone.

In pairs: think of one of your own emotional moments, where you had to find space that was right for you to be able to re-lease your feelings and then think of the process of coming into therapy, the relief of the neutrality but sometimes the coolness of the clinical setting.

    c) How might you have re-written one paragraph of that early scene to create a different picture?

2. **Stories within Stories**
    Exercise. Thumb Nail Sketch   see p166
    Discuss the technique, what it achieves in terms of focus etc, and how it is helpful for facilitating step-ping into another's shoes.

a) Write or speak in thumb nail language: for example, I am Annie. I am married to Harry. Have several peo-ple play each character and then discuss differences

Chapter 2

1. **Family Scripts. See p169**
    John Byng Hall wrote about Family Scripts. What is your understanding of this and how they can help us as therapists?

2. Thinking of the script, and your thumbnail sketches, improvise a scene from one of the following situations (don't think about it too much just get into role and try).

    a) Harry and Annie in preparation for the doctor's homecoming.

    b) Elizabeth. Think of a scene before they left for New Zealand where she and the doctor were brooding about things.

    b) Maria. Think of her staying at a friend's house and the sorts of things she might be talking about.

3. **Fleur and Maria**
    a)   What are you learning about the girls?

    b)   **Going to two separate schools.** What's your memory of school days?

    c)   **Create a referral:** Role-play a Family Therapy session with Maria, Fleur and family.

Chapter 3

1. **Family Therapy**

   a) What is your understanding of Family Therapy? How would you explain it to someone?

   b) If you were acting as a therapist what would you be thinking of in playing the part of a therapist?

   c) How do you use your own experiences to bring some bearing on the work you are doing?

2. **Relationships**

   a) Consider the impact of two sisters marrying two brothers.

   b) What unspoken concerns might Maria have if she were coming to therapy pre wedding?

   c) What concerns might Fleur have if she were coming to therapy pre wedding?

Chapter 4

1. Secrets.

a) People keep secrets, what is your view of the difference between a secret and a veiled truth?

b) What if there was another secret we don't know about? Have a think what it could be and weave a web so that when Maria comes to therapy the secret starts to be revealed.

2. Therapy

a) Fleur is on her own again. Consider her coming to therapy, and the whole thing of her only knowing what she knows.

b) Draw a family tree with her to access the information.

c) If you were Fleur what would you be hoping for from the therapy?

3. Trauma
Consider Fleur. She has had the loss of both parents and now loses Maria and Jeremy.

a) Reflect on a time when you felt you had lost everything. Think of the depth and strength of those feelings and the difficulties for anyone getting in there to help sieve through some lighter thinking.

b) Is going away always running away?

c) The Traumas. Have they made you think differently about how to handle trauma, personally and professionally.

4. Narrative.

Consider one of the titles below and write and read a paragraph announcing your new book.

Bring down the moon, a story about:

a) Broken relationships.
b) Disappointment in life.
c) Triumph over adversity.
d) Over the rainbow.
e) Strong women.
f) Negatives.
g) A Priest's confession.

Reflecting point.
With a theme from above in mind, see how you might stretch the story in different ways.

When we present cases might we sometimes be misconstruing or exaggerating pieces of information so that the case discussion starts to gather momentum picking up on things of little importance?

What safeguards can we put into place for that to be challenged?

METAPHOR Present a couple of papers on Metaphor and show it in action in the story.

Chapter 5

1. The cliffhanger moment?

a) How have the stories within stories heightened your awareness of your own? Can we ever get back to the beginning of anything?

b) Fleur is selective in what she says to Lily.

c) Consider honesty/secrets and lies and the quotation below, using a Reflecting Team discussion (Tom Andersen).

When Fleur was with the old priest, it was as if Fleur gradually managed to believe that:
'just sometimes some truths too big to hold could rest a while in the arms of the moon.' Maybe wonder with her a moment?

Does Polly walk up the path and knock on the door? Improvise a short scene that happens, and reflect.

I hope you have enjoyed using the narrative to practice your craft.

.

Bring Down the Moon

ACKNOWLEDGEMENTS

In thinking of acknowledgements it goes without saying that there will be people unmentioned who nonetheless are included in my thoughts. Please know who you are and feel valued.

GRANDPARENTS,

I want to thank them for their love, resilience and stories. To Grandmother Laura, I look at her portrait every day and thank her for so much.

WRITING.

From the early drafts of writing, there are several people I particularly want to thank:

Ray Brown: playwright, for alerting me to ways of crafting characters bringing them to life through dialogue;

Janet Foster, my friend and colleague, for our conversations about creative writing and psychotherapy;

Helen Jolly for sharing her insight into the interlocking stories and for her personal support.

 I also wish to thank:

Susanna de Vries: international author, historian. Her fascination with pioneering women is legendary, leaving a stunning imprint stopped in time, through her research and writing. Thanks to Susanna for her mix of honesty and sensitivity; for piecing together some of our family story, and for sharing the strands that have brought us together through email.

PSYCHOLOGICAL INSIGHT

No acknowledgements to my thinking would be complete without thanks to the memory of psychiatrist/family therapist: **Tom Andersen.** Some of the developments of his work around: ' seeing how we live in our words,' is so riveting, and helps to create such new possibilities in our thinking.

Special thanks to clinical psychologists/ family therapists: **Jeff Faris; Claire Collen; Ailsa Smith** for clinical supervision and support.

THE EDIITING PROCESS
Chipmunka. Thank you to them for their mission to raise awareness of mental illness within journeys and normalize the struggles of life. Thanks to :
Obiz Ogbenns
William Kettle.

Separate from the above process thanks to
The Literary Consultancy, and later from
Kitiara Pascoe, and from
Ann and Lucy for their wonderful help with content editing.

THE COVER
Zoe Grimes I want to thank her for capturing in silhouette the heart of the story.
Will for rolling the moon down into cover.
Vibrant Pulse special thanks to Dani for an upbeat website and media coverage.

LIBRARIES
Thanks to libraries for their guidance, encouragement and enthusiasm. In particular to:
Linda Paton David Pearson Julie Walker Paul Cowan Kate Gielgud Nigel Humphrey, Colin Bray, Carol Jary, and Love Reading to mention but a few.

MORAL SUPPORT. Thanks especially
Mark, and Charlie, for the chirpy contact that kept me laughing, thinking and thank you also for your impatience at times that kept me on track.

Nanette, Trevor and Maggie, son in law David, family and friends, thank you for so many things. What a welcome addition the little grandchildren are to our story:
Erin Rose and Isla Grace.

Eva Le Bon

Bring Down the Moon

Eva Le Bon

Bring Down the Moon

Lightning Source UK Ltd.
Milton Keynes UK
UKOW04f0914011013

218274UK00001B/8/P

9 781849 916462